AND
c.1

Anderson, Mary

Emma's search for
something

DATE			
			2

Emma's
Search
for
Something

Emma's Search for Something

MARY ANDERSON

ILLUSTRATIONS BY PETER PARNALL

Atheneum / 1973 / New York

A
c.1

my

Emma's
Search
for
Something

CHAPTER ONE

*I*t was a soft spring morning in early May when Emma Pigeon first realized she felt "peculiar."

She leaned down from her ledge on top of the old apartment building on Riverside Drive and glanced out dreamily over the Hudson River. The whitecaps gently swirling with the tide were gleaming in the morning sun, and a large Circle Line excursion boat headed downriver.

Emma sighed. That boat was yet another sign that spring had finally come to stay. There had been vague hints and promises of its arrival for weeks. But suddenly there could be no doubt that it had definitely established a stronghold in the city.

Riverside Drive displayed its new coat of muted greens. In window boxes all along the side street, pink and red geraniums leaned toward the warm sunlight. As if overnight, the apple blossoms by the Drive had opened up and hung heavy on the trees, while dandelions popped up in the most unlikely places. And in every branch of every tree, Emma heard the constant chirrup and chattering of her neighbors, the sparrows.

Usually at this time of year, Emma was gaily clearing off her ledge, casting out worn, useless items, and foraging for new warm-weather furnishings. Usually, she was chatting with her fellow pigeons about the long, lazy, carefree summer days that lay ahead.

But this spring, Emma felt different. Each new awakening sign of growth and change in the city made her feel slightly more uneasy. And now that she sensed everything had suddenly burst into full bloom, she felt more "peculiar" than ever. She had a strange, sad, twitchy-itchy feeling inside of her—a vague yearning she'd never felt before.

She'd mentioned the malady to her husband Clarence when they'd gotten up that morning. But he'd only shrugged his wings and said,

"Spring fever, Em. That's all it is."

Then he'd flown off to the playground for an early morning drink from the kiddie sprinkler, leaving her alone on her ledge. In fact, all the birds had flown off for either breakfast or their morning exercise.

Along with Emma and her family, the old Victorian building facing the river was home for many dozens of sparrows and pigeons. It had a large center court, which caught the afternoon sun, and a smaller back court, which protected against the chilling winter winds from the river. Across its façade, decorating the upper cornice, were twelve sculptured lions with flowing manes and bared teeth. Their noses and ears were chipped and worn in several places and they were missing a few front teeth, but still they were impressively majestic. Emma, her husband, and their children, Willie and Maude, lived in one of the choicest spots—atop the third lion from the left, on the downtown side.

Emma strolled over to the other end of the ledge and glanced up the side street. Mr. Sanchez, the superintendent of the center building on 99th Street, was busily washing down the sidewalk with his hose. Two dogs and their masters were on their way for a morning walk in Riverside Park. Some schoolchildren, their briefcases dragging, were sleepily trudging up the hill toward the West End Avenue public school.

Truly a lovely spring morning, Emma thought, and sighed again. She retraced her steps to the opposite end of the ledge and watched her children, who were looking for the remains of yesterday's picnic crumbs on the hill across the Drive. When Maude would find something, she'd gobble it up before Willie had a chance to notice. And when Willie would spy a tasty morsel, he'd do the same.

Emma was about to fly over and scold them for their selfishness, even though she knew Clarence wouldn't approve. "They're not babies any more, Em," he'd say. "Let them handle things themselves." Luckily, she stopped herself, because just then, Clarence came flying around the corner of 98th Street and would have caught her "meddling" again.

He fluttered down on top of the ledge and pecked his wife affectionately on the head.

"Isn't it a beautiful morning, Em?" he said cheerily. "I bet the park'll be jammed with picnickers today. What do you say we have lunch by the 106th Street Statue? A bunch of people who lunch out up there are on a health food kick—sunflower seeds, whole-grain breads, the works. It'd be a nice change from our sandbox cupcakes, don't you think?"

The idea didn't appeal to Emma. "I don't know," she said. "I promised the children I'd supervise their swim this afternoon. The Sanitation Truck comes down the street at twelve-thirty today and you know I don't like them swimming alone when. . . ."

"For crying out loud, Em. The kids can take care of themselves," Clarence insisted. "They're not babies any more."

"Yes, dear. I know," she said, glancing down at Willie

6

and Maude scampering on the grass.

"So that's it!" said Clarence, puffing himself out and strutting up and down the ledge, allowing the play of light to bring out the iridescence of his neck feathers. "You're down in the beak because the kids are finally flying free."

"I guess you're right," she said listlessly. "But it's more than that. I have a strange sort of—well, an *empty* feeling inside."

"Yeah, I know. You told me," said Clarence. "I'd say you had a double dose of trouble; spring fever, complicated by mother-bird blues. But cheer up. I've got a sure cure for both. I was saving this for a special occasion, but. . . ."

Clarence fluttered over to a nook in the concrete ledge and started pushing aside the paper scraps, tinfoil, and matchboxes he'd collected there. From underneath the pile, he produced a cellophane-wrapped packet containing four square crackers. He put the end of the red, peel-open strip in his beak and carried it over to his wife.

"What do you think of that?" he asked proudly, dropping it in front of her. "Untouched by human mouths. A feast fit for the gods, I'd bet. Read the label, Em, and tell me what it says."

Emma sighed again. How very like Clarence to think that mere *food* could cure all ailments. She crooked her head to one side and stared at the label, first with her right eye, then with her left, and read aloud:

"Cheesy-Squares. Ingredients: wheat, powdered milk, cheese solids, peanut butter, and grape jelly."

"Oh, darn!" squawked Clarence in disgust. "Does it really say *jelly?*"

"I'm afraid it does, dear," she said sympathetically.

"Pigeon feathers!" he shouted. "I know how jelly makes your chest itch. And here I thought I'd found you a real taste treat to cure the blues."

"Don't let it bother you, dear," she said. "I wasn't hungry anyway."

"Well, in that case," said Clarence diplomatically, "if you don't mind—perhaps I'll just take a nibble or two."

"Go ahead, dear." She sighed and looked dreamily out over the Hudson River.

Sometimes, it seemed to Emma that being able to read was nothing but a bother and an inconvenience, even though her ability had always impressed Clarence. He said she was probably the only bird in the *world* who knew how to read. But since Emma never left the neighborhood, she couldn't be sure. Though she did admit it was an unusual trait for a bird. Emma'd come to take it for granted, since reading was a talent her mother had taught her at an early age.

Emma's mother had hatched on a fire escape somewhere on the Upper West Side one cold winter morning. Her parents must have met with some dreadful city disaster, for they never returned to care for her. Luckily,

some kindly people whose windows faced the fire escape found her there the next day, half-frozen and starved. They force-fed her baby cereal and warm milk, keeping her alive by some combination of charity, luck and positive thinking. When she'd fully recovered, the family kept her as their pet, and she was given a box in the playroom to live in. The little girl of the family read her children's stories and nursery rhymes each day, and by some strange quirk of nature, Emma's mother had picked up the knack of reading for herself.

In fact, when she was fully grown and ready to leave her human home to go out into the world and mate, she had been reluctant to leave all the wonderful books behind. So, when Emma's mother had met Emma's father and decided to set up residence on Riverside Drive, she had taken with her one souvenir of her human home—a paper-bound copy of her very favorite book, *The Little Engine That Could*. When Emma had hatched that next spring, her mother had passed on her reading ability to her only child.

Unfortunately, Emma had never felt the same fascination for reading as her mother had. She had inherited the book as her dowry when she flew off to marry Clarence. But during their first winter, when the ledge grew particularly cold, Emma had to shred up several of its pages to keep warm. Then last spring when her eggs hatched, she'd used several more pages for her nest. So now, all Emma had left were the last three pages of the book, sadly yellowed and water-stained. She kept them as a fond remembrance of her mother, but rarely read them herself.

It seemed that Emma's friends were all more intrigued by her ability than she was herself. Sparrows and pigeons would occasionally come by and ask her to read a snatch of newspaper or magazine they'd found. Or on dull days, she might read the traffic signs to them. Apparently, the words ONE WAY, NO PARKING, BUS STOP, NO U TURN, held a certain fascination for her friends that it didn't hold for her.

Freddie, who lived on the seventh floor of her building and knew about her special ability, would frequently pad along the ledge and wait for Emma to fly by. In his mouth, he'd often have a torn-open letter, postcard, or telegram that he'd want Emma to read to him. Freddie was a very nosy cat and liked to know everything that went on with the people he lived with. Emma was reluctant at first, not realizing that city cats had long ago abandoned the habit of chasing city birds. But once she discovered this, she was happy to oblige.

Though for the most part, to Emma reading just meant knowing when not to eat a package of crackers, because it had "jelly" written on the label.

"Listen here, Em," said Clarence, breaking into her thoughts. He'd finished the entire package of crackers and was feeling quite mellow. "What you need is a change of scene. I've had a few cases of the old spring fever myself, so I know. Why don't you take a flight over to Central Park? You've never been there. Go for a dip in the lake, maybe. You'll feel like a new bird. I'll watch the kids and everything till you get back."

"No, I don't think I want to. . . ."

"Now don't argue," said Clarence. "Once those pretty feathers of yours are catching the breeze, you'll snap out of that funk."

"But Clarence," Emma protested. "I don't like to leave the neighborhood."

"That's part of your problem, Em," he explained. "You're in a rut. Same old ledge—same old faces. Go on now."

After a bit more coaxing, Emma shrugged and reluctantly flapped off in the direction of Central Park. Clarence sat back on his tail feathers and watched his wife fly over the bell tower of St. Michael's Church, certain he'd prescribed the proper medicine.

CHAPTER TWO

*E*mma felt a shivery feeling through her feathers as she glided toward Central Park. She never left Riverside Drive and didn't enjoy flying alone. Glancing down, she saw an area of meadows, open parkland, woodlands and thicket, murky ponds, and a reservoir, surrounded by the clutter of buildings and streets.

As she reached 72nd Street and saw the pink cherry and white apple blossoms and yellow forsythia in full bloom, plus thick magnolia petals drifting to the ground, she knew Clarence had been right. A change of scene was just what she needed.

A group of people were paddling in rowboats across the lake, and white ducks were scampering around beside the pier of the boathouse, busily eating scraps of hot dog buns and sandwiches that people threw them. Emma had never seen ducks before, so decided to join them for a little chat and perhaps a slight snack.

As she fluttered toward the boathouse, she heard a strange mixture of sounds. They were coming from a short distance away in an area called the Ramble, a hilly section with paths winding through groves of locust, willow, maple, birch, oak, and sycamore trees.

As Emma flew over to investigate, the strange sounds grew louder. At first, they were all mixed together, and she couldn't understand them. Then, each sound became separate and distinct. The sounds were definitely the songs of birds. But their calls were nothing like the chattering of the familiar sparrows and starlings she was used to.

They seemed to come from the highest branches of one tree, and hypnotically, they beckoned her closer. First, she discerned a sort of chippery *zit-zit-zz-zipa-zipa-zipa-zip-zi-zi-zi;* followed by some liquidlike music further off in the distance: *eelolah, ahlolee, oleelah, aleeloh.* Then, a clear, rich, low-pitched whistle: *aydle-tee-tee-tee-wheedle-wheedle-tay-tay;* followed by a thin, musical laughing sound: *he-he-he-he-hi-hi-ha-ha-ha.*

Could all these varied notes be coming from the throats of birds? She swooped down toward the center of an oak tree and looked up to where the calls were originating. And there, for the first time, Emma met a small section of the city's migratory inhabitants. She'd only seen an occasional robin or blackbird on the Drive, but never such a collection of different-sounding, lovely looking feathered creatures. Their muted shades of lavender and blue and their bright reds were quite impressive.

Emma had always been content with her own coloring: her soft, smoky-gray body, blending toward a darker gray about the neck and face, with a slight touch of tan at the chest and back for shading, and two white tail feathers for accent. But compared to these birds, she felt lackluster.

They appeared to be a friendly group, and all interrupted their songs to introduce themselves. Emma settled on a branch and nodded hello to all of them. There was a Tennessee warbler, a woodthrush, a Baltimore oriole, a cardinal, a summer tanager, a yellowthroat, a bobolink and a Cape May warbler. Even their names sounded exotic.

"My, I've never seen birds like any of you before," said Emma, quite impressed. "And I've lived on Riverside Drive for ages."

"Oh, we stick to Central Park," explained the warbler. "We fly-by-nights don't get over to the river much, do we gang?"

A giggly twitter went up among the group.

"You see," said the woodthrush, cocking his reddish-brown head in Emma's direction and proudly displaying the dark spots on his flanks, "Central Park is our little home away from home—our spring hotel, you might say. An oasis in the steel and concrete. But we don't hang around the city for long, so we don't get to see the sights. It's a here-today-gone-tomorrow type of deal with us. Right now, we're on our way back home."

"Where are you all from?" asked Emma.

"Oh, up-aways," said the woodthrush. "New England mostly. You know—Vermont, Connecticut, Massachusetts—places like that."

To Emma, up-aways meant flying to Grant's Tomb on 125th Street. But these places sounded so faraway and foreign, they must be in another country. Especially that one called Mazz-a-chew-pits.

"You mean you've *flown* all that way?" she asked in amazement.

"We've flown much further than that!" said the bobolink, laughing. "Personally, I've come all the way from Chile."

"Yes, it has been chilly," said Emma. "But it's quite warm and nice now."

"No. I mean Chile," laughed the bobolink. "You know—in South America."

Emma didn't know at all, but it sounded even further away than that Mazza—than that other place. "You mean you've flown all *that* way?"

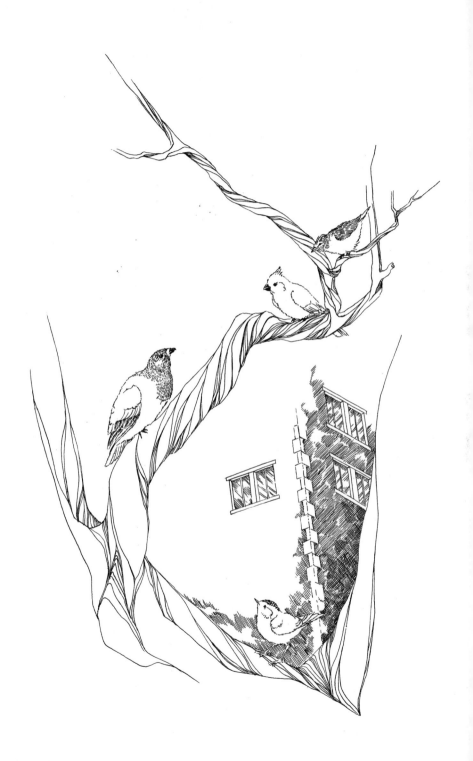

"Why of course. That's what wings are for, aren't they?"

Another giggly twitter went up from the group. But to Emma, it hadn't been a silly, obvious statement at all. In her mind, wings were for taking her from 96th to 99th Street when she was in a hurry. And many times, she could walk the distance just as well. She'd never thought her wings could transport her from one end of the city to the other, let alone to another *country*. Suddenly, that funny feeling she'd had earlier began coming back.

"Do you visit the city a lot?" she asked. "I guess you really like it here. Personally, I've always been partial to my little home on Riverside Drive, but I guess. . . ."

"Noo—twice a year's our limit," interrupted the yellow throat. "You know what they say about it being a nice place to visit, but. . . ."

"Oh, stop joking," twittered the oriole, momentarily interrupting the preening of his orange chest feathers. "The lady has obviously never met a bunch of gypsies like us before. She's used to her quiet little life on—where did you say you lived?" He turned his head toward Emma with a slightly condescending nod.

"Riverside Drive," she answered. "It's really quite lovely there. It's always been my home—myself and my family's, that is."

"Ah yes, Riverside Drive," repeated the oriole. Only when he said it, it didn't sound quite as lovely. "Well, there's no doubt about it. You city birds are a breed apart. I guess the noise and dirt of the metropolis doesn't bother you. But we migrants are different. We've got to fly free. We've got to feel that wind flapping against our wings and old Mr. Sun beating down on our . . ."

"Shut up, Lyle," shouted the bobolink. "That pigeon isn't interested in your flapping wings." He turned toward Emma. "What did you say your name was, sweetie?"

"I didn't," she said, "but it's Emma."

"Well, Emma," interrupted the woodthrush, "what Lyle here was trying to say is that we migrants enjoy traveling. We're not stay-at-home types like you pigeons."

"But what about your homes? And your nests? And your children? You can't have much of a family life," said Emma, thinking of her warm little ledge and her loving family waiting for her atop the third lion from the left.

"Our home is wherever we care to make it," explained the woodthrush. "And our children quickly learn to become seasoned travelers, too."

Emma thought about this a moment. She couldn't imagine her family ever wanting to go any further than the 97th Street playground, with its cold-water sprinklers, the sandbox filled with children's castaway snacks, and its large leafy shade trees.

"Well, I guess that kind of life is all right for some,"

she said, "if you're not happy where you were born. But as for me. . . ."

"Who said we weren't happy?" snapped the woodthrush. "My good woman, we happen to come from some of the loveliest countryside known to birds. Clear blue lakes, rolling green hills, scented meadows and valleys. That's why we're on our way back there right now."

"But if it's so beautiful, why would you ever want to leave it?" she asked in confusion.

"Let me try to enlighten you," said the summer tanager, who had been silent up until then. He was one of the smaller birds, but what he lacked in size, he made up for with his colorful red feathers and poetic speech. Leaning back on his tail feathers, he began to explain. "Ohio is my home, and most agreeable in the summertime. And I find New York quite a refreshing spring stopover on my journey back there. But in the winter, *both* grow dull and tasteless to such as myself. Great masses of snow do not stir the creative soul, so I must be off to explore new lands. I begin to hunger for the sun-baked sands of tropic shores. My wings fairly cry out to glide over the dense undergrowth. And my heart longs to see the majestic beauty ancient man has set down in those far-off places. The pueblos of the New Mexican desert. The great Mayan stone temples rising high in the center of the Yucatán jungle. The pyramids deep in the rain forests of southern Mexico. The massive citadels of granite stonework left by the Incas in Peru.

"Ah yes, there the great art is not closed up inside buildings. It's set amid nature, for all those adventurous enough to seek it out.

"Then, to fly even deeper into the denser sections of the jungle, where no man has yet left his mark. To mingle with my multicolored brothers, who are so remote from civilization, man has yet to look upon them. Where the trees and sky are alive with musical songs of joy.

"And of course, I also enjoy conversing with the splendidly plumed birds of those lands. Many a starlit night we've sat in a silent forest, comparing customs and ideologies."

"As you can see," interrupted the bobolink, "Horatio here is a bit of a culture freak. What he means is, we steer clear of cold weather. Can't find worms when snow covers the ground. Besides, if we hung around one spot all the time, we'd become as dull and ordinary as—well, we just couldn't stand it."

The bobolink caught himself before he finished his sentence, but Emma felt he'd planned to say, "as dull and ordinary as you must be."

Emma's head began to buzz with new thoughts and sights, and she grew quite dizzy. Suddenly, all the things she held most dear seemed gray and ordinary. The idea of travel and culture sounded fascinatingly tempting.

Surely, the best medicine for her "rut" would be to get some of both.

"Have you met any *pigeons* during your flights?" she asked.

"Oh no, my dear," chirped the woodthrush. "You city types have never acquired the taste for a succulent earthworm or a fully ripened mulberry. Dried-up hamburger buns are more to your liking. And goodness knows, there aren't any of those where *we* go."

Another knowing twitter went up among the birds, and Emma flushed red under her gray feathers.

"But I wouldn't worry about it," added the warbler. "The gift of the wanderlust isn't given to all. I'm sure you're quite content with your humdrum, predictable way of life and think us nothing but a pack of drifters. I bet you have a cozy little nook somewhere by that river place, that you can't wait to return to."

"Why yes, I have," said Emma. "It's atop the third lion from the left, on the downtown side."

"Sounds utterly *fascinating!*" trilled the warbler sarcastically. "On the downtown side, you say?" Then she and the bobolink began to snicker nastily to one another.

"Well, we'll be here for a day or two longer," said the tanager, giving his friends a scolding glance, "if you care to fly over and chat again. I'm always glad to meet a native New Yorker. I've set up camp in this oak tree since it suits my needs so well. It also affords a lovely view of the Museum, don't you think?"

"The Museum?" asked Emma.

"Yes, of course," said the tanager, gesturing with his right wing. "The Metropolitan Museum of Art, over there on Fifth Avenue. Quite a striking example of nineteenth-century architecture, don't you agree? But I'm sure you've visited there many times."

"Oh—certainly," Emma lied, too embarrassed to admit she'd never seen the museum *or* Fifth Avenue. There was no doubt about it. She was badly in need of cultural improvement!

"Well, I must be getting home now," she said. "My family will be waiting. Thank you for your hospitality."

"Come again," nodded the tanager. "And if you don't see me right away, just ask for Horatio."

"Goodbye Horatio. Goodbye all," said Emma, flying from the oak tree.

Emma had planned to return home immediately, but instead took a brief flight eastward, passing the sailboat pond, then going up along Fifth Avenue, toward the Metropolitan Museum of Art.

Horatio had been right, she thought. It was truly a remarkable example of—whatever kind of nineteen-something he had said it was.

with the other and read:

Dear Mr. Williamson:
Thank you for your check. It arrived this morning. I am happy to have found a place which meets with all your specifications and I'm sure you'll find the summer cottage to your liking. All new kitchen appliances were installed last season, it's a one-block walk to the beach and you may take possession on May 31st.
I hope to serve you again in the future. In the meantime, have a most enjoyable summer.

Sincerely yours,

Kenneth Rushton
Armoor Realty Agency
Martha's Vineyard, Massachusetts

"What does it mean, Freddie?" asked Emma. "Are you moving?"
"Just for the summer," he said. "We *always* try to get away in the summer."
"Oh," she said. "I guess I never noticed. I was so busy with my hatching last spring, and then with baby care all summer, I didn't have time to notice anything."
"Well, I've never been to Massachusetts before," said

Freddie. "The old folks usually take me to Long Island or New Jersey. This oughta be a pleasant change. But I wish they'd consult *me* on these decisions once in a while. If it weren't for you, Em, I'd never know what was going on in my own house."

"I met some birds from that place today," said Emma. "They told me it has some of the most beautiful countryside in the world. Clear blue hills and rolling green lakes—no, I guess it was the other way around."

"Oh, it doesn't really matter," Freddie grinned. "Once we get out of the city, I can twist those old folks right around my little paw."

"What do you mean?"

"Well," said Freddie, broadening his sneaky smile, "In the city, they don't let me out. So they never worry about my running away. But once we leave the city, they start to fight about how the 'poor animal should get out in the fresh air.' So they let me out of the house. But they're never quite sure I'll return, see? So they always put out fresh liver and broiled bluefish and fresh cream, ta make sure I'll come home at night. Naturally, I wouldn't dream of tellin' them I'm happy bein' their pet. I've gotta maintain my aloof image, ya know."

"Gee, I'll miss you, Freddie. I never realized people did so much moving around when spring came. In fact, there's a lot of things I never realized before. And it's making me feel quite strange."

"Aw, your only trouble is nothin' ta do, Em," said

Freddie, rolling over to sunbathe his sleek, shiny stomach. "I've been observing you for a long time now, what with your bein' the only nonhuman around here who reads and all. I've been studying your life style, ya might say. And I think I've put my finger on your problem. I saw a case just like yours on TV last week. You're one of those busy types. Always flittin' around, fixin' and tidyin' up things, right?"

"Yes, I guess I am," she said.

"Yeah, well now you've hit a lull—nothin' left ta clean, and no job so important it can't wait till tomorrow. So you're startin' ta feel kinda peculiar. And that's why you're in such a pickle."

"Now that you mention it, Clarence told me almost the same thing this morning. He said it was spring fever and mother-bird blues and that I needed a change of scene. But I got a change of scene over in Central Park today, and now I feel worse than ever. It made me realize how culturally deprived I am."

"Aw, forget that stuff," said Freddie, flicking a fly from his nose. "You don't wanna mess with culture this time of year. What you need is *travel*. A change of scene. Tell ya what. You and the family fly up to Massachusetts with me this summer. The old folks put out enough food to feed an army, so you won't haveta worry about starving. Anyway, I'll bet they get lots of juicy mail up there. And I hate ta think of it all going into the garbage without my knowing what's in it."

Emma shook her head. "No thanks, Freddie. You know how partial Clarence is to the city. And now that McDonald's Hamburgers and Colonel Saunders Kentucky Fried Chicken have opened up on Broadway, I don't think he'll be wanting to travel much. I'm not even sure *I* want to travel. I really don't know *what* I want."

"As far as I'm concerned, travel's the only answer," said Freddie. "Besides, this place gets me down in the summertime. The old folks don't have an air conditioner, ya know. So it gets pretty hot in that apartment. I remember one summer we were all stuck in the city. It was so darn hot, I had ta sleep out on the fire escape at night. For weeks after, I had grooves on my stomach from the iron gratings. And it took me days ta lick the soot outa my fur. No, give me a nice beach house any day. I like ta go down and dunk the old paws in the water every once in a while. And you haven't lived till you've tasted a freshly killed bluefish, broiled in butter sauce. I tell ya, Emma, there's nothing like it."

"Well maybe so," she said. "But I don't think I'm the traveling type. Until this morning, I'd never even been to Central Park."

"Yeah, Emma," said Freddie, growing drowsy from the warm sunshine and the sweet thoughts of buttered bluefish. He curled up in a corner beside the cool clay geranium pots. "I know you've always been a real homebody," he said. "But the traveling bug can hit any time.

And Central Park is better than nothing. At least there's a few lakes over there to cool your claws in."

He yawned and closed his eyes. "But if ya change your mind about Massachusetts, let me know, will ya?" Within another minute, he was fast asleep.

Emma flew back to her ledge to think about what Freddie had said. Had the traveling bug hit her? Was that why she felt so strange? Or was it because of her need for culture? After a while, she arrived at what she considered a marvelous solution to the entire problem.

Why not *combine* travel and culture? She and the family could move over to the east side of Central Park, thereby getting a change of scene without leaving the city. They'd also be close to the museum, so Emma could begin her cultural education. The idea pleased her so, she couldn't wait to discuss it with her husband.

But by the time Clarence flew back to the ledge with Willie and Maude, it was time to prepare dinner. Clarence had found a half-eaten Hostess Twinkie and two ice cream sandwich wrappers, which he set down in the center of a strip of tinfoil that served as their tablecloth.

Willie had managed to scrounge up a small packet of salted peanuts with three nuts remaining in the bottom. And Maude, flushed with pride, returned to the ledge with a sliver of peanut butter on seeded rye bread.

Dinner was the one meal the family ate together, each contributing whatever food they had found that afternoon. In the corner of the ledge, Emma kept an empty

Dixie Cup, which got filled with rainwater. This the family used both for drinking and for washing up with after meals.

Willie and Maude chattered between themselves about how busy the playground had been that day, and Clarence told the family of the adventure he'd had outside the Nedick's Luncheonette on Broadway.

"Why the place was absolutely packed," he said. "That swinging door was going all day long. And there were hot dog bun scraps falling like flies! You should have been there, Em. Roscoe the Sparrow and I could hardly believe our eyes. I tell you, all signs indicate a great summer in the food department."

Willie and Maude greedily gobbled up the last remaining tidbits of salted peanuts.

"Ma," asked Willie, "can we go over to the uptown side and play with the sparrows who just hatched? Mrs. Sparrow has a real swell nest—bits of string and yarn, two hair clips, and a strip of innersole from a sneaker. She says we can come over to play whenever we like. Can we, Ma? Can we?"

"I'm afraid not," said Emma. "You know you're not allowed to flutter about after dusk. Besides, there's something important I want to discuss with your father. And I think you should hear it too."

"What's up, Emma?" asked Clarence. "Does it have something to do with your flight today? How was Central Park? I haven't been over there in ages. I hear they've opened up a new restaurant by the Bethesda Fountain. And isn't the Tavern on the Green a great place for leftovers?"

"Please," interrupted Emma. "Can't we get off the topic of *food* for a moment?"

"Well, okay," said Clarence. "No need to get touchy. What's on your mind?"

"I've been thinking over what you said this morning. And I've decided you're right about my being in a rut. But it's not only me who needs a change. It's our whole family."

"What are you driving at, Em?" he asked.

"It's time we all spread our wings a bit," she said. "I was flying by Fifth Avenue today and noticed several choice locations on the roofs along there. I even saw some lovely garden terraces overlooking the Metropolitan Museum. Any one of them would make a suitable home for us."

"But I don't wanna move," whined Maude. "All my friends live here."

"Yeah," Willie added. "And what about my racing team? Me and the guys have a real swell club going. We race from 96th to 100th Street every day. And the winner gets to sit on top of the Fireman's Monument all afternoon—without bein' pushed off!"

"You can make new friends on the East Side, children. And there are dozens of statues in Central Park."

"Now hold it just one minute, Em," said Clarence.

"Where did you get such a crazy notion? Do you have any idea what goes on over there on the East Side?"

"What do you mean?"

"Listen, I know all about that place. It's Nowheresville for birds. Did you ever fly over those fancy stores on Madison Avenue? Know what all of 'em are? *Dress shops!* And *Dry cleaners!* Not one Nedick's. Not one pizza parlor. Nothing! And all those fancy folks pack up the minute the weather gets warm and take off for the Hamptons.

"What are the Hamptons?" asked Emma.

"East Hampton. South Hampton. West Hampton—there's a bunch of 'em. Believe me, I know all about it. My cousin Virgil spent a summer there once and nearly *starved* to death! Those rich dames leave their kids with hired nannies who never go out cause it's too hot. So there's no snacks in the sandboxes, and nothing but sour orange drink in the wastebaskets. And let me tell you about those fancy terraces. The butlers keep spraying all the bushes with insect poisons. It's enough to make a pigeon *choke!*"

"Oh, Mommy!" Maude began to whine. "I don't want to starve and be sprayed. Please say we don't have to go."

"Now calm down," said Emma. "I'm sure your father's exaggerating. Maybe there aren't any pizza parlors, but I'm sure there are other sources of food."

"Oh sure," said Clarence with disgust. "There are

loads of fancy French restaurants, where chefs dump *garlic juice* on everything. There's nothing decent to eat, and there are no garbage cans lying out in the street. The whole place is a pigeon's nightmare. You couldn't get me to move there on a bet!"

Willie and Maude started whining again about how they'd always loved their little ledge and never wanted to leave it; and how they hated the smell of garlic juice and didn't want to go anyplace where there were no garbage cans or kids or Cracker Jack or peanuts, until Emma thought she'd burst into tears herself.

"All right, children! That's quite enough!" she shouted. "I'm sorry I brought the subject up. I merely thought this family could spread its wings a bit and get some culture at the same time."

"For crying out loud, Em!" said Clarence. "You're already the most cultured bird around. You can *read!* And if you want to flit around visiting museums in your spare time, I'd be the last to object. But don't wreck our happy home!"

"Let's consider the topic closed!" said Emma. "Besides, it's time for the children to bed down for the night."

"Does that mean we don't have to move, Ma?" asked Maude pleadingly.

"Don't worry, dear," said her mother. "We won't move. I promise."

CHAPTER FOUR

*W*hen Emma awoke the next morning, Clarence had already flown off for his morning's foraging in the park. Willie and Maude were hanging over the ledge, watching the sanitation men empty out the garbage cans. They hopped up and down with delight whenever a food can or milk carton rolled out of the truck onto the sidewalk.

"You children stay by the block till I return," said Emma. "I'm taking a little morning exercise."

Emma took off in the direction of Central Park, following the same route she'd taken the day before. As she reached the big oak tree in the Ramble, she saw Horatio the summer tanager in the same spot on a high branch. All the other birds had gone, with the exception of one lavender-and-blue bird she hadn't met the day before. Next to Horatio's red-and-yellow feathers, she was a lovely color complement.

"Good morning, Miss Emma," Horatio called. "Come up and share a branch with us. I'm afraid you've missed the rest of our little group. The sky was so clear and blue this morning, they all decided to finish their long journeys home. But let me introduce a new friend. Miss Emma, meet Bernice Bluejay. She just flew into town last night."

Emma nodded hello as Bernice fluttered down from the top of the oak tree.

"Quite a flight it was, too," she said. "Nearly flew smack into the Empire State Building. Did the same thing last year. There ought to be a law against buildings that big. They're a menace to the entire bird population. I was sailing along, free as you please, when suddenly this giant steel monster popped up from out of nowhere."

"My goodness," said Emma sympathetically. "I imagine traveling has some dangerous drawbacks."

"Don't you believe it," said Horatio. "Bernice likes to overdramatize. Oh, I admit there are dangers at times, but one learns to avoid them."

"What type of dangers?" asked Emma.

"Well, any bird worth his worms knows enough never to use the Atlantic Oceanic Route when migrating. There's just too much danger in flying nonstop over the sea. We use the Atlantic Coast Flyway instead. In that way, we can land and rest when necessary."

Horatio leaned over and began to nibble the remainder of a horsefly he'd left lying on a center branch. "But excuse me," he said, "I'm forgetting my manners. Would you care for some, Miss Emma?"

"No, thank you. But I would like to hear more about your travels."

"Well, my dear. Travel is a subject I can speak of at length. In fact, my friends accuse me of becoming downright long-winded at times. But to me, there's nothing to compare to the joy of gliding over acres of pink sand, glistening in the sunlight. Or flying high over a tropical rain forest, after a shower has washed everything sparkling clean and fresh. Or soaring above in a cloudless sky, certain in the knowledge the next spot one sees will surely be more beautiful than the last. Only then can one truly know what a spectacular gift the Great One bestowed upon us, when He saw fit to grant us wings."

Emma listened to Horatio's poetry with opened beak and widened eyes.

"Wow!" shouted Bernice. "And you say *I'm* dramatic!"

"Oh, but it sounds beautiful," said Emma. "You

know, I think I've begun to get some of that traveling feeling myself!"

"You?" asked Bernice. "But you're a *city* bird!"

"I know," she said. "But yesterday, I got an invitation to Massachusetts, and I almost thought I'd like to take it. I knew it was impossible though, because of my family. Then I thought I might like to take just a little journey—from the West Side of Manhattan to the East Side. But my family wasn't too happy about that, either."

"They sound like real *swingers!*" chattered Bernice. "Can't wait to meet them!"

"Oh, they're really nice," said Emma defensively. "It's just that they're happy where they are. And so was I, until yesterday."

"I wouldn't blame them too much," said Horatio diplomatically. "Although raising a family in the city has definite drawbacks. But I imagine you've learned to be philosophical about them."

"I have?" asked Emma.

"Oh yes," said Horatio. "I'm sure you consider the noise, dirt, soot, blasting horns, and traffic jams as mere grains of sand put there to test your mettle."

"I do?" asked Emma.

"Why certainly, my dear. Now, you take the oyster. The oyster can swim along in the water quite contentedly for the longest time. Then one day, he discovers a tiny grain of sand embedded in his shell. It annoys him. It itches him. In short, it bothers him tremendously. But what can he do? He can't blow the sand out of his shell. He can't shake it out. So he must learn to live with it. And how does he do this? By constantly rubbing against that grain of sand. And every time he rubs, he covers it over with the thinnest layer of film. He persists in this endeavor, rubbing layer after layer of liquid film over that tiny grain of sand. And in the end, what has he produced? One of nature's true miracles—one tiny, perfect pearl. Your big city is like that, my dear. From out of all the dirt and noise, you, too, must learn to produce a pearl. I must admit, it's an awesome challenge."

"Sounds like a lot of baloney to me," snapped Bernice. "What would a pigeon want with a pearl, anyway. Now, if she were a colorful bird like me, she might like to wear it in her tail feathers, but. . . ."

"Im afraid you missed my point entirely," said the tanager. "I was trying to explain to Miss Emma the meaning of perseverance—something you could use a dose of yourself, Bernice. You're just as flighty a bird as I remembered you to be from last spring. Pardon the pun, Miss Emma."

"Listen, Horatio," said Bernice. "If you got any stuffier, they'd stick you in a museum. This pigeon doesn't need perseverance. She needs to kick up her claws a little and enjoy life. Whenever your type migrates to the big city, all you do is sit in a tree and eat worms.

Some life! Now *I* know how to behave in New York. I can tell you all the best spots to visit. I like to see a little action before I take off for the country."

"Have you come from far away, too?" asked Emma.

"Who me? No chance," said Bernice. "I winter in Florida. I like to cruise over the big hotels near Miami Beach. None of this roughing-it jazz for me. Horatio's the outdoors type. He loves those sweaty deserts and sticky rain forests. One year, you even flew as far as Brazil, didn't you Horatio?"

"Brazil?" asked Emma. "My, that does sound far away."

"A mere stone's throw to some, my dear. When the winter breezes fill the air, I must be off in search of the sun. I must follow it—slavishly, if you will, but it is my fate."

"Yeah, well that's not for you, honey," said Bernice. "A nice little flight down to Greenwich Village would be more your style."

"Greenwich Village?" asked Emma. "I've heard of it, of course, but I've never actually been there."

"What did I tell you," said Bernice. "Bet you've never been to Coney Island either. You New Yorkers are all alike. Listen, I'm flying down to the Village right now to see an old pal. Why not come along?"

"Well, I don't know," said Emma. Bernice looked a bit irresponsible, and she wasn't sure it was wise to spend much time with her.

"You said you wanted a change of scene, right?" said Bernice. "Besides, the big outdoor art show just started, and a friend af mine'll probably exhibit his paintings."

"Well, if it's to be a *cultural* afternoon," said Horatio, "I suggest you go along, Miss Emma."

Trusting Horatio's judgment, Emma agreed, and she and Bernice flew off downtown.

CHAPTER FIVE

*E*mma was exhausted by the time she and her new friend reached 14th Street. Her wings were limp and weary from flying such a long way, and her ears were ringing from listening to Bernice's constant babbling.

Throughout the flight, Bernice bragged about what a brilliant, beautiful bluejay she was. Since Emma hadn't met any bluejays before, she wasn't sure if they were all this vain. But she suspected Horatio was right. Bernice was a very "flighty" bird.

"Can't we stop and rest a moment?" asked Emma,

thoroughly out of breath.

"Don't be silly, honey. We'll be there in another minute. See Washington Square Park down there? We'll just keep circling till I spy my pal, Maurice. I bet he'll be thrilled to see me."

Bernice had already told Emma all about Maurice, the terribly talented, though struggling, New York artist.

Emma glanced down and saw a large stone arch facing up Fifth Avenue. There were two statues beneath it on either side and children were dangling their feet in the center fountain. There was a park surrounding the arch and a playground toward the back. Further on were stone chess tables with several old men seated around them playing. Good Humor wagons were being pushed about the busy area, but most of the activity was taking place on the narrow side streets and avenues outside the park.

On each corner, artists were sitting on deck chairs, their paintings resting alongside buildings and against cars and lampposts; even propped up on boards along the street. They practically covered every sidewalk.

The birds flew down lower to glimpse the paintings. There were some in ornate frames and others on stretched canvases. There were watercolors, oil paintings, portraits, still lifes, seascapes, and animal art. One artist had painted everything on black velvet and another had glued seashells onto weathered old boards.

There were also heavy metal sculptures twisted into funny curlicue shapes and little tables where young people were selling handmade copper and ceramic jewelery. Through the tiny path down the center of the sidewalk, hundreds of people were strolling by, examining the works of art; some stopping to admire a particularly lovely exhibit, others bargaining with artists over the prices of things.

"Maurice isn't at his usual spot," said Bernice, hovering over the top of a building on 8th Street. "Last year, he set up his stuff right there on Fifth Avenue. That's one of the choicest locations."

Emma looked down. There was a fat old woman wearing a big white hat seated there now, with a collection of cat portraits. There were cats of all colors and sizes, from cuddly kittens to tough-looking alley cats.

"Yucch!" squawked Bernice disapprovingly. "Who'd want to buy a picture of a stupid old cat."

Emma thought the paintings quite nice, but Bernice just shrugged her feathers. "Once you've seen Maurice's work, you'll know what a true artist can do. Listen, I know where he lives. Let's fly over to Houston Street and see if he's at home."

Emma much preferred to sit on the roof and watch the passersby, but Bernice insisted, so they took off again. They flew several blocks west, until they came to an old, run-down brick building on a dingy-looking street.

"That's Maurice's studio, right there," said Bernice, pointing her beak in the direction of a dusty window on the fifth floor of the building. They swooped down and settled on his ledge.

The window was partially open and Bernice stuck her head underneath the window frame.

"That's Maurice, right there," she said. "Doesn't he look creative?"

Emma peeked in the window. Busily painting at an easel was a very tall, slender man, with long orange hair down to his shoulders and a bushy red-brown beard. He wore a beat-up pair of dungarees and a tattered shirt, both of which were covered with paint. He was putting the finishing touches on a painting of a large bird. The bird was unlike any other Emma had ever seen before. It had a beak bigger than its entire head, with streaks of yellow, blue and green painted on it and splotches of bright colors all over its feathers. Surely such a bird must have been dreamed up from the imagination of a great artist, thought Emma.

She bent her head down further and peered at the dozens of other paintings scattered around the sparsely furnished room. They were *all* of birds. Tiny fragile shore birds feeding at the edge of sandy beaches, great gray-and-white gulls flying high over the ocean; and land birds, some flying, some resting, some nesting, all so realistic, Emma felt they might fly off their canvases at any moment.

"See?" whispered Bernice. "I told you he's a great artist. He's a regular bird nut. He paints nothing else. He's done a portrait of me, you know. I bet it's worth a million."

"Really?" asked Emma. "It must be wonderful to have someone paint you."

"It's not bad," she said nonchalantly. "I was passing by New York last spring and happened to settle here on Maurice's ledge. When he saw me, he practically had an attack. Thought it was some good-luck omen or something. Artists are strange like that, you know. Then he got out a book that told what bluejays eat. Well, it must have said something about our liking corn, because before I knew it, he'd run down to the store and gotten me a whole stalk of the stuff. He left it out on the ledge for me, so's I wouldn't fly away. And for the rest of the day, I hung around while he painted my portrait. It was so good, he put it in the art show."

"How exciting," said Emma. "He's made you famous."

"Yeah, well, an artist knows true beauty when he sees it," she said. "Now watch me give him another thrill. Wait till he sees I'm back again."

Bernice lifted her head and in a series of mixed warbles and twitters, called, "*Meeiah-meeiah-heetolay-heetolay-tolili-tolili!*" over and over again, until she'd gotten Maurice's attention.

Quickly, he turned from his canvas and ran toward

47

the window to open it further. Bending down, he slowly put out his hand in greeting.

"Why, it's my bluejay," he said softly. "Could you be the same little spring bluejay?"

Bernice twittered softly once more, turned her head toward Maurice, then blinked her eyes several times. Emma sat on the far edge of the ledge and watched. Bernice was actually *flirting* with the man. She postured and fluttered and strutted and ruffled up her feathers so their lavender and blue caught the soft sunlight. She even batted her eyes every now and again.

Maurice began to laugh. "You *are* the same little bluejay!" he said excitedly. "There couldn't be two like you. How have you been, my friend?"

Bernice leaned over slightly and let him smooth down her soft chest feathers. Then he extended one finger, to coax her onto his hand. "Come on now, my love," he said softly. "Come into my studio and I'll show you your portrait."

Bernice acted shy and coy for just a moment, then hopped willingly onto Maurice's finger. He was about to close the window, when he noticed Emma seated on the other side of the ledge. He swooshed his other hand in her direction, and with a scowl on his face, said, "Shoo. Out of here, you pigeon!" then slammed the window shut.

Emma fluttered around the ledge in a state of confusion. She couldn't understand it. She was a bird, too!

Why didn't Maurice make a fuss over her? She settled down on the ledge again and peeked through the closed window. Maurice was sitting on an orange crate, stroking Bernice's feathers. He placed her on the floor, then began going through a pile of canvases in the corner until he came to one in particular.

It was a large portrait of Bernice, her head held high, as she perched atop a stalk of golden corn. Bernice cocked her head from side to side, admiring her likeness, which pleased Maurice greatly. Then he walked to the corner of the room and took a bowl from his cupboard, placing it on the floor beside Bernice. Emma couldn't be sure, but it looked as if it was filled with shelled nuts.

It was then that Emma realized she, too, was hungry. She tapped on the window with her beak, but Maurice didn't notice.

Emma began to realize what a bad mistake she'd made flying off with Bernice in the first place. The afternoon sunlight would soon be fading. Her family would be waiting and worrying. And she didn't even know the way home.

Though the ledge was growing cool, there was nothing for her to do but wait. Maurice would have to open the window sooner or later. She looked inside the room again. Bernice had just polished off the last of the nuts and was beginning to blink her eyes again. Emma sighed and waited.

She watched the sunlight fade even more, and still she waited. A flock of sparrows flew overhead, but just as she was about to ask them directions, they swooped round the other end of the building and were gone.

"Oh, what a foolish bird I am," muttered Emma. "If only I'd learned to travel sooner. If only I knew my way around the city. If only. . . ."

Maurice's window opened, and Bernice flew out onto the ledge.

"Goodbye, my springtime gypsy," he called, blowing her a farewell kiss.

Bernice quickly rose up over the top of the buildings, never bothering to glance back to see if Emma was following. Emma quickly flew to catch up, but since Bernice was such a seasoned flyer, it was difficult for her. At one point, Bernice dipped down behind a high rooftop for a moment, and Emma feared she'd lost her. Then suddenly she saw the familiar splash of blue flying in front of her again.

"Bernice!" Emma called. "Wait for me!"

"Oh, hi honey," she twittered. "You still hanging around? Thought you'd left hours ago."

"Well, I was waiting for you," she said. "What were you doing in there with Maurice for so long?"

"Oh, nothing much. He gave me a little snack, and then he chattered about art for a while, and showed me all his paintings. Say, what did you think of my portrait? Personally, I don't think he did me justice. I have a much better profile."

"No, it was just lovely," said Emma. "All the paintings were lovely. But for a person who loves birds so much, he certainly was rude to *me*. He practically pushed me off his window ledge! Is that what you meant by artists acting strangely?"

Bernice gave Emma a questioning glance. "You certainly didn't expect him to treat *you* nicely, did you?" she asked. "Why, you're a *pigeon!*"

"I don't understand," said Emma. "What's wrong with being a pigeon?"

"Oh, honey! You've got to be kidding!" Bernice exclaimed. "People don't like *pigeons*. Even *bird-lovers* don't like pigeons! Nothing personal, but pigeons are as common as dirt. You saw all those paintings in Maurice's room, didn't you?"

"Yes."

"Well, there were gulls and terns and cardinals and wrens and thrushes—just about everything. But," she asked mockingly, "did you see any pictures of pigeons?"

Emma thought a moment. "No, I don't think I did," she said.

"Well, there you are," snapped Bernice. "Pigeons are just too ordinary to bother about."

Bernice's words reached Emma like a cruel slap in the face. The bluejay turned round and flew faster toward the 59th Street entrance of Central Park.

"It's all your own fault, you know," she said. "You

let people take you for granted. All you pigeons are alike—hanging around the streets, camping out on buildings, eating gutter castaways. Humans get sick and tired of seeing you. But when a robin or a cardinal or a lovely bluejay, like myself, comes to town, they practically fall out their windows trying to catch a glimpse of us in their binoculars. You've got to play hard-to-get if you want humans to notice you. Besides, you don't even know how to sing. You can't expect people to get excited over a dirty street bird who doesn't even sing! Maybe if you washed yourself up a bit, got some manners, and learned a tune or two, things would be different."

"Why are you saying all these terrible things to me?" asked Emma. "I thought you were my *friend!*"

"Look honey, I happen to think you're a real nice pigeon. But let's face it, you're still just a pigeon. The lowest form of bird life. But that's the breaks, sweetie. We can't all be special, you know."

They flew the rest of the way in silence, and when they reached the West 79th Street entrance of the park, Bernice turned a wing and waved.

" 'Bye now, honey. And think over what I said. Maybe you could take some music lessons. And a bath wouldn't hurt either!" Then she flew off into a cluster of trees in the Ramble and was gone.

Emma rested on a bush for a moment before continuing home. She never flew at night, and dusk made the landmarks seem strange and unfamiliar. Heading uptown, she finally glimpsed the top of the bell tower on St. Michael's Church off Amsterdam Avenue, and knew she was just two blocks from home.

She saw her spot on the ledge coming into view. Clarence, Willie, and Maude were all awaiting her. The children were hanging dangerously close to the edge of the building, listening for some sign of their mother's return.

"Where have you been, Mommy?" screeched Maude, as Emma settled down with a rustle of feathers. She was dusty, disillusioned, and thoroughly tired out.

"Yes, Em," said Clarence, with more than a trace of annoyance in his voice. "The kids and I've been going half crazy all day. We even checked all the side streets and flew over the West Side Highway. We thought you might have gotten hit by a car or something."

"That's right," whimpered Maude. "Willie said you'd probably been squished up under a big truck."

"I did not!" Willie shouted. "I said I hoped she *wasn't* squished."

"Anyway," Clarence interrupted, "you can see we've been worried to death. Where on earth were you?"

Emma was much too weary to explain. She yearned for a long rest on her peaceful ledge. But feeling she owed her family some explanation for having been gone so long and worrying them all so, she recounted her day's adventures, beginning with her chat with Horatio.

"And he winters in Mexico and Yucatán," she explained. "Doesn't that sound exotic?"

"Who wants to go to a place called yucchy-tan," Willie giggled.

Emma gave him a disapproving glance. "And he told me about the cool rain forests and sun-baked sand," she continued, "and the excitement of flight and—oh, all sorts of lovely things."

"That's swell, Em," said Clarence, unimpressed, "but I don't see any difference between those places and our own Riverside Park."

"How can you say that?" asked Emma. "I'm talking about living with a sense of adventure."

"I know it," he said, "but *our* lives are filled with adventure, too. Some days, I take my life in my beak just walking along inside that playground. Between the tricycles, kiddie-cars, wacky-wheels, and ten-speed bikes those kids whoosh around on, I'm lucky I haven't had all my claws trampled into the cement by now."

"But that's not the same thing at all," said Emma. "I'm talking about true adventure and *discovery*."

"Just try dodging those kids' slingshots! You'll find out all about true adventure," he snorted. He puffed out his chest and began hopping quickly back and forth, as he always did when he got excited. "And the discovery of a half-eaten slice of pizza on the grass is all the discovery I need, thank you very much!"

"I don't think you understand the traveler's soul,"

Emma said, sighing.

"Yeah, well maybe you should stay away from that whole crowd. They're not like us, Em. They don't understand city life or city birds."

"Well, you're right about that, dear," said Emma, then told him about her trip downtown with Bernice and the dreadful things she'd said about pigeons.

"What did I tell you!" fumed Clarence. "The nerve of that bluejay. If she'd said that to me, I'd have pulled out every feather in her fresh little head. 'Common as dirt,' are we? Why, she's nothing but a country bumpkin. We pigeons have a noble history. You'll find us in every big city in the world. We live near the most famous spots, too: museums, statues, buildings. And I'll match my coo against her chattering any day."

"Calm down, dear," said Emma. "Had I known it would upset you so, I'd never have told you."

"Well, I'm glad you did," he said. "It just proves my point. I know it was my idea you fly free for a bit, but I think you've had enough. I want you to promise me not to visit those gypsy birds again. They mean nothing but trouble. Ever since you've met them, there've been weird ideas in your head. Yesterday you wanted to move to the East Side; today, it's Mexico. Lord knows what you'll want tomorrow!"

"But I would like to say goodbye to Horatio," said Emma. "He's quite a gentlemanly type—not at all like Bernice."

"Nosiree," Clarence insisted. "The kids and I want you to steer clear of Central Park from now on. Isn't that right, kids?"

"That's right, Mommy," Maude shouted.

"Yeah, Ma," said Willie. "We don't want you getting squished!"

"All right," sighed Emma, "I promise."

She was too tired to argue any further. She fluffed up her dusty feathers, tucked her head beside her chest and closed her eyes.

CHAPTER SIX

*E*mma was awakened the next morning by raindrops softly falling on her back. She shook her feathers and promptly woke her children before they got soaked. Willie grumbled when he noticed the bad weather, complaining he'd have to miss out on his afternoon race, and Maude whined that she hadn't finished sleeping.

Clarence instructed his family to fly to the shelter of the building's eastern court, where the cornices overhung a few extra inches, protecting them from wind and rain. Once they'd all settled down, he began a heated argument with Roscoe the Sparrow about whether it was a spring shower or the beginning of a true storm.

"See those whitecaps out there on the river?" chirped Roscoe. "That's a sure sign bad weather's brewing."

"Nonsense," said Clarence. "Bet it doesn't last more than ten minutes. They'll be plenty of picnickers in the park by noon."

"I don't know," said Roscoe skeptically. "I think our best lunch bet would be a trip over to West End Avenue. Some guy had a big party up there last night. Kept me up half the night with his noisy records. There's sure to be potato chips and popcorn in the trash cans this morning. Maybe even some cheese dip."

"Can't stand cheese dip," said Clarence. "Always has onions or garlic stuff hidden in the middle."

Emma found their conversation more boring than usual. She was wondering what Horatio was doing now, and if the bad weather would cause him to stay over in the city a while longer. She even wondered what nasty Bernice was up to, and was sorry she'd promised Clarence not to see them again.

But Clarence was right. They meant nothing but trouble. Her brain had been full of strange ideas and longings ever since she met them. Yes, she was better off sticking close to home and her safe, predictable life on the ledge.

Still, she couldn't help feeling life lacked something.

If only she knew exactly what it was!

Then just as suddenly as it had started, the rain stopped, and Willie and Maude flew down to the playground to chat with the sparrows.

"How about a trip to the bakery, Em?" asked Clarence. "The delivery truck's due about now. If we're lucky, the driver might drop a loaf of bread. Or maybe a prune Danish. I know how partial you are to Danish pastry."

"No, thank you," Emma sighed. "I'm not hungry."

"You're not mad about last night, are you?" he asked.

"No, dear. I'm just tired. Perhaps I'll take a nap in the sun, now that it's come out."

So Clarence took off to forage, and Emma sat in the warmth of the afternoon sunlight. There was a large freighter anchored in the Hudson. Emma squinted her eyes to read its name. *The Brazilian Titan.* Had it sailed past the same exotic places as Horatio? she wondered. When autumn came again, would it trudge down the Amazon River with Horatio flying high above it? Would it pass cool jungle rain forests and come to shore off sun-baked sands? She blinked her eyes, and with a half-yawn, half-sigh, nodded off to sleep.

When she awoke, it was already evening, and Clarence was seated beside her. The children had been safely tucked in for the night, and he'd set up their tinfoil tablecloth in front of the ledge. On it, he placed half a slightly soiled prune Danish, a sizable chunk of sesame seed roll, and one soggy chocolate-chip cookie.

Emma blinked her eyes and smiled at her husband. He was really awfully sweet at times.

"We've got a regular feast tonight, Em," he said softly. "I sent the kids off early. I thought we'd have a moonlight dinner—just the two of us, like we used to, remember?"

"That was thoughtful of you, dear," said Emma. She was quite hungry now and began pecking at the Danish pastry.

"Told you the bakery was a good bet," he said proudly through his stuffed beak. "The sidewalk was slippery from the rain, and the delivery man fell in a puddle. I got there just in time to take advantage of it. Sure beats Roscoe's cheese dip."

"Very resourceful of you," said Emma, gulping down the last bit of Danish and starting on the sesame seed roll.

"This is the life, isn't it, Em?" asked Clarence, puffing out his blue-green chest. "There's no place like New York City. Look out there at the West Side Highway. All those headlights flashing through the night, like a year-round Christmas tree. And that gentle buzz of car motors is more restful than any music. And way uptown, the lights from the George Washington Bridge, like a necklace of precious jewels sparkling in the distance. Is there anything more beautiful in all the world?"

Emma nodded in agreement. But what she was really

looking at were the lights from the freighter *The Brazilian Titan,* and she was still wondering about those lush jungles, cool rain forests and sun-bleached sands of the tropics.

Even when she'd finished eating, she had an awful empty feeling somewhere inside.

* * *

Early the next morning, Freddie the Cat was sitting out on the fire escape, *pssssstting* again. He was dangling a magazine from the corner of his mouth, and when he *pssssstted,* it would slip from one corner to the other.

"Hey Emma, come down a minute," he said.

Emma flew down to the seventh floor, and Freddie dropped the magazine on the grating.

"I saw the old folks reading this yesterday. Said it had something about Martha's Vineyard in it. Read it to me, will ya?"

Freddie turned the pages with his paw until Emma noticed the caption, MARTHA'S VINEYARD, VACATION WONDERLAND.

"It's a long article, Freddie," she said, glancing at the two pages of printing.

"Look it over and skim the cream off for me, all right?"

Emma read through the article and capsulized the highlights.

"It says it's a storybook island resort, with sailing, swimming, fishing, golfing, and fancy shops. Thousands of people vacation there every summer."

"Darn it!" said Freddie. "Sounds like a real tourist trap to me. I hate spending the summer in a tourist trap."

"What kind of trap?" asked Emma.

Freddie stretched out along the grating to explain, using his right paw for an occasional conversational emphasis.

"Well, I'll tell ya. A tourist trap is a place that starts as a real swell deal—lots of trees, clean water and stuff. Until lots of people start finding out how great it is. Then all of a sudden, they start showin' up with transistor radios, funny beach hats, and crazy colored shirts. And before you know it, the good stuff starts going down the drain. That's what this Vineyard place sounds like. I'm not sure it's the spot for me. No indeed. I like to commune when I go away."

"Commune?" asked Emma.

"Yeah, sure. You know. Commune. With nature. Summer's my only chance to do it, when I get out of the city. Can't do much communing on this fire escape, ya know. But like I said, once a place starts fillin' up with night-club joints and pinball machines and stuff like that, nature goes right down the drain! I spent a summer in Atlantic City once, so I know."

"I see what you mean," said Emma. "But you don't

have any choice, do you?"

"Maybe I do," he said slyly. "I could always come down with a case of hangnail or severe fur ball at the last minute. Naa, I guess not. Then I'd be stuck in *this* joint all summer."

As he rolled over to consider the problem, a breeze blew by and sent the pages of the magazine turning. As it did, Emma noticed a large picture of a bird on one of them. It had a beak bigger than its head, covered with yellow, blue, and green splotches.

"That's just like the bird Maurice was painting!" she said with surprise. "I thought he'd made it up, but it must be real. I wonder what it's called."

"Read it and find out," said Freddie.

"The bird's name is toucan," said Emma as she read. "It's part of a new bird exhibit called the World of Birds, which just opened at the Bronx Zoo. It says all the birds are in their natural habitats."

"Is that good?" asked Freddie.

"I think it means they've surrounded them with things they know and like," she continued. "This toucan lives in the South American rain forests. And they have other rare and exotic birds from all over the world. And they're not in cages. It's sort of like a big room where they fly around for people to see."

"Sounds like a dumb idea to me," said Freddie. "They'll all probably fly right out of the place."

Emma read further. "No, Freddie," she said. "The

birds don't want to fly out. They're very happy inside and think it's their real home. And the keepers feed them all their favorite foods."

"Not bad," said Freddie, after a moment's consideration. "Maybe I'll go *there* for the summer."

"It's not quite the place for a cat," Emma smiled. "But it's *just* the place *I* want to see. I've learned a lot about the tropics lately and I'm dying to see what they look like. And I'd love to speak with a bird who looked like *that*."

With the end of her beak, Emma pushed the magazine over toward Freddie. He studied the toucan's picture.

"Yeah, well this guy sure has a big nose. He must crush bones with it or something. Personally, I don't think he's worth a trip all the way to the Bronx, though."

"Perhaps not," said Emma. "Especially since Clarence has forbidden me to talk to strangers."

Freddie's ears perked up at that. "You and your old man have an argument?" he asked. Since Freddie loved gossip and Emma needed someone to talk to, she told him the whole story of the past few days. He was particularly interested in the part about Bernice.

"You say she vacations in Miami Beach, eh?" Freddie certainly had a one-track mind!

"That's not the point," said Emma, steering him back to her immediate problem. "Once Clarence heard I'd been insulted, he insisted I not speak to outsiders any more."

"But these zoo birds are different," said Freddie. "Sort of like visiting dignitaries, ya know. Visitors from a foreign land and all that. Clarence couldn't mind you're talking to *them.*"

"You think so?" she asked hopefully.

"Why sure. You'd be 'cementing domestic relations.' That's what they always say on the news when the mayor meets some visiting foreigner at the airport. Then he gives him the key to the city, and they all go out and eat chicken croquettes and lima beans."

Emma thought a moment. "*I* have a key," she said. "It's just a rusty old mailbox key I found in the street, though."

"That's good enough," said Freddie. "You could tell them it was the key to the Pigeon's Palace or something. They probably don't speak English anyway. Who's to know."

"I certainly would like to learn about South America," said Emma. "Even if I can't ever go there. But I don't know how to *get* to the Bronx!"

"It's not far," said Freddie. "I been there once. The old folks took me to see some friends of theirs. Threw me in the old traveling case—the 'hot box' I calls it. Then we all got on the subway."

"But I can't go on the subway."

"Yeah, well maybe you could fly along above it or something."

"Sounds a bit risky to me," said Emma. "But I'm

dying to see that rain forest."

"Why sure," said Freddie. "Once you've got this thing out of your system, you'll feel like your old self again."

Emma considered the plan thoughtfully. It had definite possibilities.

CHAPTER SEVEN

*E*arly the next morning, Emma and her family were awakened by Roscoe the Sparrow chattering away on their ledge.

"Hey, you guys," he said, nervously nipping Clarence in the tail with his beak. "New neighbors are moving in today."

Clarence quickly sat up. "Who are they?" he asked with interest. He was the official welcoming committee for new birds to the building.

"A young couple, just setting up housekeeping," said Roscoe. "They planned to live over on a brownstone by Amsterdam Avenue. But they're tearing it down to put up a new high-rise."

"That's progress for you," snorted Clarence. "Well, I better get over and show them the lay of the land. Are they pigeons or sparrows?"

"Pigeons. And the missus is expecting. Any time now, I'd say. She found a real nice place on the east court. But if you ask me, she's the nervous type. Keeps looking at all them air conditioners hanging out the windows. Thinks her little ones'll get sucked up in 'em."

"She's not making her nest on top of an *air conditioner*, is she?" asked Emma with concern.

"No," said Roscoe. "She set herself up under one of them cornices, so she's safe enough. Just a little anxious, I guess."

"Can we go say hello?" asked Maude. "I could bring the Mommy a piece of my yellow yarn for her nest."

"Yeah," Willie added. "And if she has a boy, I'll let him play with my piece of rubber ball."

"That would be nice, children," said Emma. "And perhaps we could have them over for dinner this evening. But first, I must get the ledge straightened up a bit. I haven't cleaned in days. Clarence, you take the children over and introduce yourselves. I'll see to the housework and finding something special for dinner."

"Okay, Em," said Clarence, pleased to see his wife her usual cheerful self again. "That's a swell idea. A new mother pigeon to talk to will do you a world of good."

With Roscoe close behind, Clarence and the children flew off to make their introductions. Cooing softly to herself, Emma hopped around the ledge, pushing the bits of paper and twigs to one corner. New neighbors will be such fun, she thought.

From the crevice in the corner, she took out her napkin, placed it in her beak and began dusting off the concrete. Then she set about straightening her family's possessions in a neat row along the back of the ledge: the weathered white twig Willie had picked clean when still a baby, the pink stone she'd found in Riverside Park, the cork Maude had seen floating in the Hudson, the pine cone Clarence had plucked off a discarded Christmas tree last winter. She piled them in a corner next to her last three pages of *The Little Engine That Could*, then picked up Willie's collection of flip-tops from aluminum cans and dropped them, one by one, into his paper cup. Lastly, she picked up her rusty mailbox key and set it on top of the rest. As she did so, she glanced at the words of the book she knew so well. "I think I can. I think I can. I think I can."

She picked up the rusty key and stared at it a moment, as yesterday's conversation with Freddie came back to her. The key to the city! The excitement of new neighbors had made her forget wanting to go to the zoo. But now that she'd remembered, the desire grew stronger

in her than before.

It seemed a far more exciting way to spend a day. How could one compare meeting two pigeons with meeting those wild and beautiful birds of the rain forest? she thought. She quickly dropped the key, feeling a tinge of guilt for such disloyalty. But the idea wouldn't leave her.

She knew Clarence would be busy all morning, show-ing the new arrivals around the street. He'd probably take them over to the playground and introduce them to everybody, then give them a guided tour of Chicken Delight and Nedick's; maybe even brag a bit about the choice location. She was sure he wouldn't be home for hours. She'd never even be missed.

She glanced down at the words of her book again. "I think I can. I think I can. I think I can."

That settles it! she thought. I will!

She flew off the ledge and headed uptown. In her hurry, she forgot to bring along her rusty mailbox key.

*   *   *

Emma could almost feel the excitement tingling through her feathers as she flew above the West Side Highway. She still had no idea of how to get to the zoo, but it didn't seem to matter any more. She was too filled with expectation.

When she reached 125th Street, Emma noticed a

huge flock of starlings underneath the viaduct. Their clear, squeaky whistle filled the morning air: *free-free-free-hay ee oo–tchikikako-tchikikako*, they called, chattering away by the hundreds. Emma swooped down to ask directions.

"Excuse me," she said. "I'm on my way to the zoo."

The starlings continued their incessant chatter, never stopping to notice her.

"Excuse me," she said again. "Could you tell me. . . ."

"Wellwhatisit? Wellwhatisit?" squeaked a group of the birds.

"I'm on my way to the Bronx Zoo," said Emma.

"Wellgoodforyou! Wellgoodforyou!" they said, and fluttered to the top of the steel pier to join the others in another raucous song.

"But I don't know the way," Emma shouted above the din. "Could you tell me which direction to fly in?"

One old starling looked down and gave Emma a beady-eyed glance. "Why, east of course, ya ninny," he said. "Fly east, then head uptown. You can't miss it."

"Flyeastyaninny! Flyeastyaninny!" squeaked several of the younger birds, joining in.

Emma thanked them, then quickly flew off in an easterly direction. She was unaccustomed to long flights and after about twenty minutes, her wings began to ache a bit. She considered stopping for a rest when suddenly she saw what looked like the zoo in the distance.

Below her were acres of green trees and grassy paths. Dotting the green landscape were smaller areas with tiny lakes and scattered ponds. And covering it all were large beasts and animals, some of which Emma had never seen before. She'd seen pictures of lions and bears and seals, all of which were below. But there were other animals too. One large creature with an unbelievably long neck and spots all over it; and another that resembled a horse, but with stripes all around its body.

Emma circled the park several times, taking it all in. Along with the animals there were hundreds of people. People looking at the animals, feeding them, talking to them, and thoroughly enjoying them.

Remembering her reason for coming, Emma started to look for the World of Birds. There were several structures scattered throughout the zoo area, so Emma decided to walk along the grounds a bit, and read the signs outside each building.

Hopping along, she noticed a sign in front of a funny-shaped building: the World of Darkness. Emma couldn't imagine what was inside, but it didn't sound friendly. She took another path and passed a great white rock with two brown bears sleeping in the sun. Even though they were fast asleep, it made her a trifle nervous.

Then she saw it. A strange, lovely shaped building with ramps jutting out in either direction, reminding her of the wings of a bird in flight. The sign said THE WORLD OF BIRDS.

Dozens of people climbed the ramps, all eager to get through its revolving doors. But how would Emma get in? There was only one way. She scampered over to a crowd of people heading toward the entrance and walked beside their feet.

There were many people and twice as many feet, so there was little room for Emma. Once, she nearly got stepped on by a large basketball sneaker. Then she was knocked in the tail by a sharp high heel. She even had ice cream dripped on her by the owner of two sandaled feet. But somehow or other, she managed to squeeze through the revolving door, along with the mass of humanity, unnoticed and without serious injury.

Once inside, she kept close to her group and followed their lead. It was difficult to see anything because there were so many legs obstructing her view. Whenever all the feet would stop, so would Emma.

"Oh look," she heard a lady say. "The New England Forest. Isn't it lovely?"

Emma craned her neck to see, and someone spilled popcorn on it. The crowd of feet shuffled along to the next exhibit. Before they were replaced by a new group, Emma hopped up onto the brass partition pole to have a look.

It was as if she were gazing through a large window, but there was no glass. Inside a shadow-box area, she saw evergreen trees, lacy lime-green ferns and tiny sprinkles of water trickling against cool gray rocks. A

75

skylight roof filtered soft morning sunlight through the branches. Throughout the area she could hear the gentle songs of birds. She recognized some of the calls as those she'd heard in Central Park and saw a woodthrush scamper from behind some leaves. The names of all the birds inside were listed on a plaque: WOODTHRUSH, BALTIMORE ORIOLE, HOUSE FINCH, SAVANNA SPARROW, and TUFTED TITMOUSE.

Just then, another group of people began pushing their way toward the exhibit, and Emma hopped back down to the floor. Which way was it to the rain forest? she wondered.

A small boy, echoing her thoughts, shouted, "I wanna see the jungle thing, Mommy. Which way is it?"

"I think it's in the next room, Johnny," said his mother. "Come this way."

Emma followed the mother and child and just missed getting her tail feathers caught in the heavy steel door. Once inside, she felt she'd truly been transported to another place. Even the temperature was hotter, and the air moist and humid. A long ramp rose up from the center of the large enclosed area, and bright artificial sunlight beat down on everything. Thick dark trees rose up to the ceiling and smaller ones with great elephant-sized leaves lined the sides. To the left, a waterfall spilled over great slabs of gray rock, and smaller trickles of water sprayed a dewy mist on all the leaves. The ground was covered with velvety moss, swampy waters, and dense vegetation.

So this was the rain forest, thought Emma. Yes, it really was lush and lovely. No wonder birds traveled hundreds of miles to reach this exotic place.

"Oh, look," sighed a woman standing beside her. "See, up there, perched on that waterfall. It's a quetzal."

Emma looked up, too, and saw a strikingly beautiful bird, with a crested head, bronze-green back, and crimson-and-white underparts. But the most magnificent part was his tail. It was longer than its entire body, with over two feet of shimmering jade-green tail plumes.

"The Aztecs worshipped that bird, Johnny," explained the woman. "They considered him the God of the Air."

Emma didn't know who the Aztecs were, but she was sure they were right. I'd love to speak to him, thought Emma. I'll just fly up there and welcome him to New York City. I can tell him all about Riverside Drive, and he can tell me about his homeland.

Emma left the crowd of pushing feet and flew up over the ramp. She fluttered about for a moment, then settled on the edge of the waterfall, close to the beautiful quetzal.

"Hello," she said politely. "My name is Emma, and on behalf of the New York pigeons, I've come to welcome you to our fair city. I meant to bring you my mailbox key, but I'm afraid I flew off without it."

The bird turned toward Emma with a graceful sway

77

of his neck but said nothing.

"You do speak English, don't you?" she asked.

Still the bird said nothing.

Emma tried another approach. "The truth of the matter is," she continued, "I've been rather bored lately. Dissatisfied, you know? I've been considering taking a trip. I've heard about your lovely country, and hoped you'd tell me more about it."

She moved closer to the quetzal, and suddenly the bird grew frightened and nervous. It leaped off the edge of the rock and began to fly about, its wings batting frantically.

"Don't go," said Emma, flying after it. They made a circling pattern around the room.

"Look at that, Harriet," shouted a man in the crowd who was watching. "Isn't that a—yes, it's a *pigeon*." He began to laugh, pointing Emma out to the others.

"How on earth did a pigeon get in here?" asked one young woman.

"Is the pigeon going to hurt the other bird, Mommy?" a little boy asked. "Don't let the pigeon hurt the pretty birdie."

Before long, the entire crowd was staring at Emma as she followed in pursuit of the quetzal. She heard their excited talking, but had no idea what all the fuss was about.

"Someone get a keeper or a net or something," shouted one man. "I think that pigeon's gone berserk."

"Maybe it's got rabies," suggested one woman. "It looks to me like it's foaming at the mouth."

The little boy started to cry. "I think that mean old pigeon is going to hurt *all* the pretty birdies." He buried his face in his mother's skirt and sniffled.

The quetzal finally flew into the safety of the high trees, where several other birds were perched. As they popped their heads out from behind ferns and leaves, Emma saw their sudden splash of brilliantly colored feathers—red, green, yellow, orange. They all stared at her with menacing dark eyes, then retreated even further into the maze of branches.

Still Emma pursued them, circling around the tops of trees, desperately trying to poke her head through the branches. But under the canopy of vegetation, their strongly contrasting plumage actually made them blend with the shadows of foliage and sunflecks, so that as long as they remained still, Emma found it impossible to see them. She squinted her eyes for a moment to protect them from the blazing artificial skylight. When she opened them again, she saw a toucan, his hard, weaponlike hooked beak pointed toward her face. Then the majestic black crest of a curassow popped out of the underbrush. Then another foreign face, and another, all rising up in a unison of violent caws and ear-splitting noises. In a band, they swooped down to the lower swampy area to defend the platter of fruits and berries the keeper had placed there.

The onlookers stood, still staring at the strange sight. "It's a disgrace!" one woman yelled. "Millions of dollars were spent to erect this gorgeous building to house exotic birds. And already it's being overrun with pigeons off the streets."

"I only see one pigeon," said a man standing next to her. "I'd hardly call that overrun."

"Just wait and see," snapped the woman. "Now that you've got *one* pigeon in here, they'll come by the hundreds. There's no getting rid of them. They're worse than roaches!"

"What's the trouble here?" asked the keeper, pushing his way through the heavy steel door.

"That filthy pigeon is terrorizing these beautiful birds," the woman shouted. "You have to do something about it immediately!"

Meanwhile, Emma was still vainly striving to communicate with the frightened birds.

"Don't be afraid of me," she pleaded. "I'm a pigeon— a bird, just like you. I may not look quite the same, but that's no reason. . . ."

Suddenly, she felt a strange sensation across her back and found herself rolled up in a ball. There was something wrapped around her entire body and she couldn't stretch her wings. Crisscrosses of string were wrapped around her, and a knot pulled up tight against her face kept her right eye closed, with only her beak pointing out through one of the holes. A young man was peering

81

down at her, the crowd of people standing behind him, and Emma knew she was caught in some sort of net.

"Wonder how it got in here?" asked the keeper, staring at her as if she were some strange specimen.

"Are you gonna kill it?" asked the little boy.

"Of course not, son," said the keeper. "We'll just throw it out on the grass. Lots of pigeons scrounge around out there. But we can't have them in here with these *special* birds."

"Yeah," said the little boy. "Pigeons don't belong with *pretty* birds, do they?"

"As far as I'm concerned," said the woman, "pigeons don't belong *anywhere!*"

"Well," said the keeper, "pigeons *are* a little different."

The keeper carried Emma outside and dropped her by a grassy area where elks were grazing, a few yards from the World of Birds.

"There now," he said, letting her free. "You'll be all right here. Just don't try sneaking in *there* again."

Emma dropped to the ground and scuttled behind a rock. And there she cowered, brooding against its scratchy brown surface.

Hours went by. The shadows lengthened, and the air grew cool. A numbness had settled over Emma, and she felt a heavy lump inside her chest. She knew she must return home before dark, so by sheer instinct, she began flying toward home.

Buzzing through her head were the vicious, taunting words she'd suddenly come to realize must be true:

"Pigeons are different—mean dirty pigeons—common as dirt! Pigeons are different—mean dirty pigeons—common as dirt!"

Over and over again, the words mocked and haunted her. And each felt more painful than if a stone had been hurled against her soft gray body.

CHAPTER EIGHT

*E*mma was a different pigeon by the time she returned to her roost. A deep depression had totally overcome her.

Again, Clarence was anxiously awaiting her arrival. Only this time, the new neighbors were waiting alongside him.

"Why Em," he said, with a sigh of relief. "We thought you'd never get here. I was just telling the new folks you'd gone out for something special for dinner. Guess you ran into a little trouble, eh?"

Emma flew to the furthest corner of the ledge and

sat down in silence.

"Uh, well," said Clarence nervously, "it's good you're back." He could see something was troubling his wife, but didn't want to bring it up in the presence of company.

"I guess I better make the introductions," he said. "Emma, meet Gilbert and Monica Pigeon—the new folks."

Gilbert nodded hello, and Monica fluttered her wings a bit and cooed, "You have such a lovely home here, my dear. Your husband's been showing us your charming possessions. I hope my roost will be half as tasteful as yours. I'm afraid I'm not very handy about the house."

"Nonsense," said Gilbert. "You have a positive flair with twigs and things." He glanced over to Emma. "She's really quite creative. But since she's been expecting, she hasn't felt like doing much housekeeping."

"Oh, Emma'll be glad to help out until your eggs hatch," said Clarence. "Won't you, Em?"

Emma stared out at the Hudson River and said nothing.

By now, even the neighbors were aware of the awkward silence of their hostess.

"Well," said Gilbert, "it's been quite a busy day for us. We'd better start bedding down."

"But you haven't had dinner," said Clarence. "I guess Emma couldn't dig up anything special, but we do have a few crusts left from yesterday, if you want to take potluck with us. Right, Em?"

Still, a dead silence from Emma's direction.

"Well," said Monica, nervously clearing her throat. "We're really not very hungry this evening. That piece of cone we found outside Carvel satisfied us quite nicely. And besides, I believe your wife looks a trifle tired. So we'd best say goodnight."

They said their goodbyes to Clarence, politely nodded in Emma's direction, then flew off to the other side of the building.

"Well," fumed Clarence, assured they were gone, "you certainly made a swell impression on those new folks. And you the wife of the Official Greeter. What's the matter with you? Do you want those pigeons thinking we're *antisocial?*"

"It doesn't matter what they think," said Emma. "They're only pigeons."

"What d'ya mean by that?" asked Clarence. "They seemed like real nice folks—just as good as us."

"Don't you see?" she said. "We're *all* only pigeons. As common as dirt!"

Emma stared at her husband with sad wet eyes, then slowly turned, sighed, and looked out into the dark distance.

* * *

The next day, Emma was no better. She refused to leave her roost, wouldn't speak, wouldn't eat; she wouldn't even go watch the children take their morning shower.

By evening, Clarence's anger of the day before had changed to a growing concern over his wife's condition. Since Emma refused to discuss what had happened to cause this depression, he was at a loss to know what to do for her.

Willie and Maude noticed their mother's strange attitude.

"What's the matter with Ma?" asked Willie. "She's been actin' real funny."

"Has she eaten jelly again, Dad?" asked Maude.

Since the weather had turned warmer, Clarence explained that Emma was feeling some ill effects from the temperature change, and this seemed to satisfy the children.

But when the second day turned into the third, and the fourth into the fifth, Clarence grew more concerned. Emma refused to speak to anybody. She never left the ledge and took only a few drops of water and an occasional scrap of bread, which Clarence brought her. Her feathers began to lose their lustrous sheen and softness, and she'd lost a good deal of weight. Still she sat, silent and uncommunicative. And always, there was that foggy, faraway, half-deadened look in her eyes.

Then on the sixth day of this unexplained behavior, Emma took a slight turn for the better. That is, she began to watch the children play their games and returned to some meager, halfhearted housecleaning. But she never left her roost and relied on Clarence to forage for all their food. She engaged in minor conversation with her husband, but refused to discuss any of the events of that fateful day.

Clarence sensed how deeply troubled in spirit his wife still was, but he couldn't guess the grave degree of her depression.

For Emma's world had suddenly shattered. Her sense of pride, dignity, and identity was gone. The things she'd held most dear now seemed contemptible. The life she'd once cherished was suddenly meaningless.

How foolish she'd been to think travel or acquiring some smattering of culture could solve her problem. The ailment that had begun to beset her mind earlier in the spring, was now all too clear:

She was the lowliest of creatures—a bird without song, without true flight, with no heritage beyond that of the dirty city sidewalks. A useless, unnecessary bird, shunned not only by mankind, but those of her own kind. A blot on the landscape. In short, a foul and filthy pigeon!

A sickness for which there was no cure! A stigma that held no hope for reversal.

As Emma sat brooding, she offered up a silent prayer that her husband and children might never come to know her humiliation, and vowed never to be the one to tell them.

With any luck, they could live out their lives in contented ignorance. How she longed for the days when she had done the same!

CHAPTER NINE

*T*he lovely warm spring days continued. Monica Pigeon gave birth to two lovely girls, whom she named Priscilla and Nan. Willie and Maude took a fancy to them immediately and spent many happy hours "pigeon sitting" while the parents went to forage. Clarence and Roscoe the Sparrow made their daily visits to McDonald's and Nedick's, and all the pigeons and sparrows enjoyed the carefree sunny days on the Riverside Drive ledge.

All but Emma. She had been in seclusion for more than three weeks. Concerned neighbors would periodically ask the exact nature of her ailment and condition. Clarence gave vague answers, from "spring fever" to "slight headache," assuring them she'd be up and about in no time.

One morning while Emma was in her usual state of lethargy, Freddie the Cat gave out with a loud *pssstt* from the fire escape.

"She can't come down," Clarence called, leaning over the ledge.

"She still feeling under the weather?" Freddie asked.

Clarence nodded his head and flew down beside the cat. "I'm afraid so," he said.

"Wow, I wish she'd snap out of it," sulked Freddie. "The old folks' mail's been piling up like crazy. And I'm gonna *leave* in a couple of days. I sure would like to know what's in all those letters before I go."

Clarence had been reluctant and embarrassed to discuss his wife's true ailment with his fellow birds. But knowing Freddie had a personal interest in Emma's recovery, he thought the cat might be of some help in finding a solution.

"If only I could figure out what's troubling her," said Clarence. "I'm sure it has something to do with that day she flew off without a word, because she hasn't been the same since."

"Ya mean that day she went to the z . . ." Freddie caught himself in the nick of time. "I mean the day she went somewhere?"

Clarence eyed him suspiciously. "Do you know something about that day, Freddie?"

The cat was silent, unwilling to admit he'd encouraged Emma's ill-fated flight.

"Well, maybe she did mention some little something about a trip," he said evasively. "But I'm not sure she went."

"Where did she say she was going?"

"If I tell ya, promise not to blow your stack, okay?"

"Come clean, Freddie," said Clarence sternly.

"Well she wanted to visit the new bird house at the Bronx Zoo and talk to all those foreigners up there."

"I knew it!" said Clarence, hopping back and forth. "I knew it must have something to do with those out-of-towners. And these are foreigners, no less. Emma hasn't been right since she met any of 'em. I should have put my foot down the minute she started talking about moving near Central Park to get culture."

Freddie was silent again. He didn't care to inform Clarence he'd encouraged her in that, either. "Yeah, well I told her nix on that culture stuff. But she was determined. Even after the way that bluejay treated her."

"You know about that, too?" asked Clarence.

"Oh sure," said Freddie. "If you ask me, I wouldn't be surprised if Emma's suffering from an acute case of inferiority. She's probably got a complex by now."

"You may be right," said Clarence, suddenly beginning to fit the pieces together. "When she came home that night, she said something about being 'just a pigeon.' You figure those zoo birds snubbed her, too?"

"It's possible," said Freddie, stretching out on his back. "In my experience, most birds can't be trusted." He turned and gave Clarence a wide grin. "Except pigeons, of course. I've always loved pigeons. Especially cultured pigeons who can read."

Clarence kept hopping from one edge of the fire escape to the other. "I think that's the answer," he said. "Emma's got that complex thing you said. But what can we do to cure her?"

"That oughta be simple," said Freddie. "Ya give her lots of compliments and stuff. That's how they handle it on the soap operas. Just tell her what a smart bird she is. You know, lie a little."

"But that's all *true*," said Clarence. "She *is* the most cultured pigeon in these parts."

"Then, that's your angle!" said Freddie. "Tell her what a brain she is. Play up the fact she can read. Ask your friends to do the same. Before long, she'll be thinking she's a genius and stop moping around."

"It just might work!" said Clarence excitedly.

"Why sure," said Freddie, rolling over and swatting a fly with his tail. "But listen. See if you can hurry it up, okay? 'Cause if she recovers in the next two days, she can read my mail."

CHAPTER TEN

*C*larence wasted no time in setting his plan into motion. He flew from ledge to ledge and roost to roost, informing everyone of his campaign to cure Emma's blues. By that afternoon, he'd visited every nook and cranny of the building and talked with every sparrow and pigeon residing there. He explained how his wife had been suffering from an acute case of inferiority and needed the support of all her friends.

Everyone seemed willing and eager to help, and Clarence assigned them all the same duty: go out and forage for writing. Snatch up every piece of printed matter you can find and bring it to Emma's roost.

By that evening, birds were descending from all four corners of the building with bits of matchbox covers, magazine ads, torn newspapers, snips of cardboard boxes, plastic wrappers, candy packages; anything with a word, or even half a word, printed on it. They asked, begged, even implored Emma to read them all.

Emma was amazed at their sudden craving and didn't know what to make of it. She sighed wearily at first, explaining she didn't feel up to the effort. But when the birds insisted, she softened and agreed.

They oohed and aahed as she read the castoffs, then thanked her profusely and returned to their roofs. But the next day, the same group returned with a new collection of packets and snippets to be deciphered. Emma found this epidemic most unusual and asked why the sudden interest in such matters.

"Oh, reading's such a wonderful gift," cooed one of the pigeons. "And you're the only one of us that has it."

"Yes," agreed a sparrow. "We just love to know what's written on things. But none of us can figure it out."

"We'd forgotten your unusual talent, Emma," explained a pigeon.

"Yes, a most unusual talent," agreed another.

"We could listen to you read for hours," sighed a tiny sparrow.

And the praise continued. How wonderful and gifted and talented and *special* Emma was, and how they all wished they could be just like her.

Clarence sat on the sidelines, cooing proudly, occasionally smiling and saying, "That's my wife! The most cultured pigeon in New York City. She even owns a book, ya know."

"Oh, a book!" exclaimed the birds. "A real book?" They chattered admiringly. "Emma actually owns a book of her very own!"

"And her mother knew how to read, too," Clarence added.

"Why, you must come from a very special family!" tweeted a sparrow.

At first, Emma dismissed their lavish compliments, still feeling the pains of her unfortunate encounter at the zoo. But as the days went by and still birds came to her roost to praise her and have things read to them, she slowly began to believe what they said. After all, she *was* the only bird with such a rare talent. Surely that set her apart from the rest of her kind. And didn't she owe it to herself and her family to make use of her gift? If this ability were hereditary, perhaps she could pass it onto her children. Then they, too, could rise above the sordid level of common pigeon!

She was certain flighty Bernice didn't know how to read. And those rude foreigners who lived in the jungle had probably never *seen* a book. How different their

reaction would have been had they known of her unusual ability. How thoughtless of her to have wasted it for so long.

Gradually, the cure Clarence had sought began to take effect. Within days, Emma was back to her normal self again, cooing and cleaning and supervising her children's playtime. In fact, she was more active than ever, hopping about the ledge, inquiring after her neighbors' health, and offering to read for them. Unfortunately, Freddie didn't reap any of the benefits because he'd already taken off for Martha's Vineyard in his "hot box."

But everybody else got more than their share of Emma's time. She never realized her friends had created this "reading ruse" purely for her benefit, and no one told her, since none of them wanted to hurt her feelings, fearing a relapse. So they humored her by still collecting their matchboxes and newspapers and candy wrappers, smiled patiently, and thanked her for enlightening them as to their contents.

But it wasn't long before things started getting out of hand. Emma began to take her reading duties a bit *too* seriously. She would leave the roost before cleaning was done, to fly off and read a magazine article to a sparrow who would much rather have taken a nap. Or she would forget to forage for dinner because she was so busy explaining to a fellow pigeon the ingredients on the discarded wrapper of the cupcake he'd just eaten.

Her fellow birds were becoming exhausted trying to keep her supplied with new reading material. Even Clarence had to agree that his wife had gone overboard. So one night, when Emma and the children were asleep, he called his neighbors together on the eastern court for a conference.

"Listen, Clarence," said Roscoe the Sparrow, nervously. "Emma's a great gal, but this has got to stop. She's got me so busy looking for gum wrappers, I don't have time to look for *food!*"

"That's right," added Gilbert Pigeon. "This cure of yours seems to have backfired on us."

"I know how you feel, folks," said Clarence apologetically. "And I agree. But we can't just tell Em to quit reading to us. It would hurt her feelings."

"Well, maybe you could get her to taper off a little," Roscoe suggested. "She doesn't have to come around every darn day, does she?"

"Yes," Monica suggested. "Perhaps she could read to us once a week instead."

"So we could get some *rest!*" grumbled Sanford Pigeon, the oldest of the group.

"I think we're taking the wrong approach," said Gilbert. "The reason we're all so exhausted is that we have to find new stuff for Emma to read every day, right? But if we could lay our claws on a *book*—well, that would keep her busy for weeks! And she could read a little bit to us every once in a while."

"A *book?*" snorted Roscoe. "Are you nuts? I have a hard enough time trying to carry a wrapper. I'd break my beak on a whole book!"

"Anyway, where could we find a book?" asked Monica. "I've never seen one on the grass or even in the trash."

"Maybe we wouldn't have to find one," said Clarence, suddenly inspired. "A few years back, I used to hang around a big building downtown on 42nd Street. Some old guy used to come there every day and feed us pigeons at 12 o'clock. I heard that he died last year, though."

"What's that got to do with anything?" demanded Roscoe.

"This building was a library," explained Clarence. "A place filled with thousands, maybe millions of books."

"Ya mean we've all gotta move to a *library?*" asked Roscoe.

"Won't do it!" muttered Sanford. "I've been living here since I was an egg and I ain't gonna move now."

"I know that," said Clarence impatiently. "But maybe we could send Emma to the library."

"Well that's better," said Sanford. "If *she* moved, we could *all* get some rest!"

"*No one* has to move," said Clarence. "Just visit. Now that Emma's got the habit, she really enjoys reading. I bet she'd read just for herself, even if no one asked her."

"Great," said Sanford. "Then we won't ask her any

more. I'm glad that's settled. Now let's get some sleep."

"Not so fast," said Clarence. "You've all gotta promise to listen to her read once in a while, okay?" There was a slightly pleading note in his voice.

"Sure we will," said Gilbert, "but only once in a while, understand?"

Clarence agreed, and the meeting was adjourned.

CHAPTER ELEVEN

*T*he next day, Clarence began phase two of his campaign to cure Emma. He was afraid he'd have some trouble convincing his wife to fly free again, but his fears were unfounded. Though he didn't know it, Emma had begun to get bored with the limited literature of gum wrappers and soda pop tops. How could she hope to raise the cultural level of her family with such mundane fare?

So when Clarence suggested a trip downtown to the library, she was intrigued. True, her long convalescence had made her wary of traveling again, but she felt she owed it to her family. If she could teach her children some of the learned things written down in books, no one could dare call any of them common as dirt again.

Early that morning, she and Clarence shared a light breakfast of white bread crusts. Then Clarence gave her detailed instructions on how to get to 42nd Street and Fifth Avenue, affectionately kissed her on the cheek, and wished her well.

Emma's wings felt a bit brittle as she flew the first few blocks. They'd gotten badly out of shape from lack of use. Gliding toward the east end of Central Park, she became aware of how long her confinement had been. The sultry days of summer had already overtaken the city. Gone were the spring blossoms and varicolored newness of greens. In their stead, the trees had a uniform appearance, and no breeze rustled their leaves. An overall hazy heat filled the air, and large sections of the grass lay parched and brown from lack of rain.

People strolled through the park at a much slower pace now, and dogs chose to lie sleepily beneath shade trees instead of tugging eagerly at their leashes. Even the men behind the ice cream carts pushed them along with only a halfhearted interest.

When she reached 42nd Street, Emma saw several people resting and talking quietly on the high stone steps in front of the immense library building. Guarding the doors were two stone lions, quite unlike the ferocious, toothy beasts who decorated the cornices of her

Riverside Drive home. These lions were more the calm, intellectual type, unaffected by the sultry weather.

The library building took up two city blocks and was quite an impressive sight. Emma circled the great structure several times, glancing in the windows, looking for the best place to position herself. Her heart pounded faster at the thought of all those books awaiting her; all that knowledge that would soon belong to her, and to her children.

But she soon realized that all those books were closed tightly, resting neatly in numbered shelves. How was she to read them?

Circling the building again, she came upon a window with an ample ledge to support her. She looked inside and found it to be just the room she required. A large sign in the center said REFERENCE ONLY, and there were long wooden tables scattered about its four corners. Several people were seated around the tables with stacks of books in front of them. Luckily, there was such a table right next to Emma's window. A young woman was seated there, with a pile of books beside her.

Emma found that by crooking her neck just slightly, she was able to read over the woman's shoulder. An ideal arrangement, except for a few problems. The woman's reading ability was more advanced than her own, so Emma had to sound out several unfamiliar words, and the book was a difficult one. Emma never quite managed to finish the page before the woman turned to the next

one. Also, her choice of reading matter was not exactly what Emma had hoped for.

All the books dealt with the same subject: a man named Leonardo da Vinci, who lived in a place called Italy a long time ago and painted lots of pictures. Hardly a topic to arouse her interest, but she had little choice. All the other tables by the windows were empty.

So Emma sat the entire morning, gaining considerable knowledge about the Italian painter. About one o'clock, she grew hungry and flew off to the park behind the library. There she found the passersby to be most generous and feasted on peanuts and popcorn and the residue in a Coca-Cola cup.

When she returned to the library ledge, the young woman was buried in another book on the same subject. Emma read along until about four o'clock, then decided to leave. She wanted to be sure to be home well before dusk.

That evening, Emma's neighbors, (grateful for an entire day's rest) stopped by to inquire about what she'd learned. She happily informed them of everything. Sitting up straight and tall, and in parrotlike fashion, she recited a barrage of facts she'd committed to memory. She had to pause occasionally to recall a word, and she mispronounced more than a few. But for the most part, she remembered it all.

"In 1466, Leonardo moved to Florence, where he entered the workshop of Verrocchio and came into contact with Botticelli, Ghirlandaio and Lorenzo di Credi," she said proudly, then paused for a breath. "While at Lodovico's court," she continued, "Leonardo worked on an equestrian monument to Francesco Sforza."

Her friends listened wide-eyed.

"What's she talking about?" whispered Roscoe the Sparrow. "I ain't understood a word of it."

"Neither have I," cooed Monica Pigeon. "But it sounds very nice."

"Maybe it's some foreign language," suggested Sanford Pigeon. "Sure don't sound like English."

". . . At Urbino, he met Niccolo Machiavelli. Bernardino Luini, Cesare da Sesto, and Sodoma assimilated from Leonardo his 'sfumato' technique. . . ."

"How much longer's this gonna last?" Sanford grumbled. "It's given me a headache."

". . . With a few swift strokes of his pen, scientific precision, and consummate artistry. . . ."

"Hey," whispered Roscoe, "*that* part sounded almost like words. I think she's telling us about some guy who makes pens."

"Ballpoint pens?" asked Sanford. "They're no darn good. See 'em in the trash all the time."

As Emma continued her recitation, the scattered whispering and mumbling steadily grew. What was she saying? What did it mean? Willie and Maude made a valiant effort to keep their eyes open, but couldn't help nodding off to sleep.

"Ahmmm," said Clarence, clearing his throat nervously, "perhaps we've heard enough for one night, Em. After all, you've had a hard day and need your rest."

Emma had grown so enthralled by the sound of the words, she'd forgotten she didn't understand half of them, either. That didn't matter anyway. She'd read them, and knew them, and tomorrow she'd read more. She barely noticed her neighbors' departure, as one by one they fluttered off to their roosts. When they'd all gone, Emma stretched herself and sighed, a warm glow of accomplishment inside her. She drifted off to sleep, with visions of books dancing in her brain.

She returned to the library early the next day, and the day after that. The fourth day was Sunday, and the library was closed. On the fifth day, the young lady studying Leonardo didn't return. But a teenage boy took her place at the table by the window. His books were all about crustaceans (shell-bearing fish). That night, she told Clarence what she'd learned.

". . . The larger crustaceans include the lobster, crayfish, crab, shrimp and barnacle."

At least this topic was of some slight interest to her husband.

"I had part of a fishburger once at McDonald's," said Clarence. "I wonder if it was made with a crus-whateveritis."

"Perhaps," said Emma. "All crustaceans have bilaterally symmetrical bodies covered with a chitinous exoskeleton."

"This one was covered with ketchup," said Clarence.

"Perhaps that's the same thing, dear," she said. "I'll find out for you tomorrow."

But the boy studying shellfish didn't return the next day, and the table by the window remained empty. Emma sat all morning, waiting for someone to fill it. But no one came. Emma tried reading over the shoulder of a man at a center table, but it was too far away to see anything. Still, she waited till four o'clock hoping someone would eventually come. She was quite disappointed to return to her roost, no smarter than when she'd left that morning.

"Don't worry," said Clarence, "I bet there'll be someone there tomorrow."

And so there was. An old man researching the nineteenth-century whaling industry in New England. And the next day, someone studying foreign diplomacy, international treaties, and protocol. Then, a man reading about engines—gasoline engines, steam engines, gas turbines.

Emma had about decided the world of books, though culturally enlightening, was a trifle dull. But the next day, the woman who came to the table by the window changed all that. And though she'd never know it, she also changed Emma's life!

CHAPTER TWELVE

*F*ate had brought the woman to the library! Emma was convinced of that. Yes, fate had placed her at the corner table with that wonderful, marvelous, glorious pile of books—all about BIRDS.

The first day, she and Emma read about sparrows. When Emma returned home that evening, there was more than a faint twinkle in her eye. And when Roscoe flew by to chat, she couldn't resist the temptation to put him in his place.

"What freaky foreign facts have you learned today, Emma?" he asked.

"Well, they may be freaky, Roscoe," she said coyly. "Especially since they were all about *you*."

"Me?" he asked.

"Yes. And they were most enlightening. I learned your ancestors come from England. And we pigeons should beware of you. You've been known to pluck out our feathers when building your nests."

Willie and Maude, who were listening, nervously sat down on their tail feathers to protect them.

"Aw, what're you talking about?" asked Roscoe. "I ain't ever done such a thing!"

"It was right there in the book," said Emma haughtily. "I also learned that for 400 years, sparrow pie was quite a tasty dish in England."

Emma chuckled to herself as Roscoe flew off in a huff.

"Is that stuff really true?" asked Clarence.

"Why, certainly," said Emma.

Then she told Clarence about the stack of bird books the woman had read, and how eager she was to return to the library on Monday to learn more. On Monday, the woman read about birds' songs and birds' calls. And the day after that, she opened the biggest book of all. To Emma's extreme delight, it was all about PIGEONS.

How she wished Bernice were there to see it. It would have turned her blue feathers green with envy. The biggest book on the shelf was about pigeons, whom she'd accused of being "common as dirt." Even Emma was surprised to learn how much there was to know about her ancestors. As she sat reading, her chest swelled up with pride. She could hardly wait to return home and share the knowledge with her family, and she was quite out of breath when she arrived at the roost that evening.

"Clarence!" she cooed excitedly. "You won't believe it. Such wonderful things. Such very wonderful things. I could hardly believe them myself!"

"Calm down, girl," he said, "and tell me what you're talking about."

"The lady in the library read about pigeons today. And the book was so fat, she only got to page seventy-five. And there are hundreds more pages to go. All about us. Isn't it wonderful?"

"Somebody wrote about us?" asked her husband, still confused.

"Not you and me exactly," said Emma. "But our grandparents."

"Somebody wrote a book about Gramma?" asked Willie, more confused than his father.

"No dear," explained Emma. "But it's a book about pigeons. Where we came from. What we like to eat. Where we live."

"Aw, we *know* all that, Mom," said Maude. "We come from this ledge, and we eat Hostess Twinkies and Cracker Jack. . . ."

"Don't you understand?" asked Emma. "It's about our *heritage!* I *knew* we had a heritage. Bernice didn't think so. She almost had me believing it, too. But it isn't true, so don't you believe it for one minute. We're truly a noble bird. There are pictures of us in the ancient caves of prehistoric man. I bet even Horatio doesn't know *that*. You see, early man considered us *sacred*. And in India, they still do. We appear on coins and stamps all over the world. There's even a statue built just for us in a place called France."

"As far as I'm concerned," said Clarence, chuckling, "*all* statues are for us."

"But this is different," said Emma. "This is a statue *of* us, don't you see?"

"Can't say that I do," said Clarence. "But if it makes you happy, it's okay with me."

Emma was annoyed that Clarence didn't share her excitement about their newly found heritage, but it didn't dampen her enthusiasm. The next day, she returned to learn even more fascinating facts. And when she flew back to the ledge that evening, she had a dreamy, languid, faraway look in her eye. Clarence offered her a share of the leavings in a potato chip bag, but she merely smiled and said she wasn't hungry.

"You feeling 'peculiar' again?" he asked with concern.

Emma sat smiling and muttering to herself. "Such brave, noble birds. Who would have believed it?"

"Did ya learn some more stuff about us today, Ma?" asked Willie.

"Oh yes, son," she said, drawing him closer. "And I

want to share it with all of you."

So her husband and children settled beside her as Emma recounted what she'd learned.

"First, I found out all about the famous people who've bred us."

"Lots of people give us bread," Maude interrupted. "That nice old lady up the street leaves some on the grass by the service road every morning, and that man. . . ."

"No, not that kind of bread, dear," explained her mother. "I mean pigeon breeding—people who've had us for pets. There was Queen Victoria, who was a famous ruler, and Mary, Queen of Scots, and King George. And a famous lady who wrote poetry named Elizabeth Barrett Browning. Bernice may have been painted, but we've been *bred!*"

"That's real nice, Em," said Clarence, "but. . . ."

"I haven't come to the best part yet," Emma interrupted. "Next, we read about racing homers. Most people refer to them as carrier pigeons, but that's not their proper title. Likewise, the words pigeon and dove are often confused because the Germanic word, *Taube*, was the same for both. Now, our direct ancestors were called rock doves because they made their homes on the edges of cliffs. Therefore, we're extremely well suited to live in big cities filled with giant buildings so similar to those cliffs."

"Yeah, that's super, Em," said Clarence, growing

more fidgety, "but what's that got to do with . . ."

"I'm coming to that, dear," said Emma. "Racing homers, or carriers, are almost the same as rock doves. In fact, we look *exactly* the same. There were dozens of pictures of them in the book. In fact, one of them looked just like my Aunt Edith. And carrier pigeons have always been popular with humans because they make such fantastic heroes."

"Heroes?" asked Clarence, his ears perking up at last. "You mean. . . ."

"No, dear," said Emma, anticipating his question. "I don't mean hero sandwiches. I mean brave noble pigeons who fought, yes and even *died,* in the cause of duty."

"Wow! Tell us about it, Ma," said Willie, truly interested for the first time.

"Well, dear, carrier pigeons, or homing pigeons, are your relations. They're trained to fight in the armed forces, along with the soldiers."

"Really?" asked Maude. "Do they wear helmets and carry guns like the people on the statues in the parks?"

"No, dear. But they're just as brave. There was one bird named G.I. Joe who fought in a place called Italy. That's where Leonardo da Vinci lived, you know. But this was not as long ago. 1943, the book said. Well, some enemy soldiers had taken over a town called Colvi Vecchia and the good soldiers wanted to bomb it. But then the good soldiers captured the town and wanted to tell their fellow soldiers not to bomb it, after all. But they couldn't get word to them. So they sent G.I. Joe instead. They tied a message around his foot, and within twenty minutes, he'd flown twenty miles, stopping the bombers just seconds before they took off. He became so famous, he was even awarded a medal."

"A medal?" asked Willie, wide-eyed. "Of his very own?"

"And there was a lady pigeon who became famous during that war, too," said Emma, turning to Maude. "Her name was Lady Astor. And another pigeon fought in another war. His name was John Silver. They called him that because there's a famous book with a man with one leg. But this pigeon lost his leg fighting for his country. But, oh, my favorite story of them all was about *Cher Ami*."

"Tell us about him," said Willie, still enthralled.

"Well, Cher Ami fought for the French soldiers a long time ago. One day, a French battalion advanced too far and was surrounded by the enemy. Several pigeons were released to send an SOS back to headquarters. But they couldn't get through. The bullets and gunshells were flying heavily, and they all fell dead. All but one—Cher Ami. With the message attached to his foot, he flew through all the shells. Even after the guns had shattered one of his legs, still he flew, until he reached his home loft. The bullet that had torn away his leg had also pierced his breast, and the message was hanging from what was left of his shattered leg. But that day, Cher Ami saved an entire battalion of soldiers. And when he died, they took his body and put it in a big museum in a place called Washington. He became so famous, a lady wrote a book all about him."

The children sat wide-eyed and fascinated. "Gee, Ma," said Willie, "that's the best story I ever heard."

Clarence was more skeptical. "Sure it isn't a fairy tale?" he asked. "How come I never knew about this stuff? I don't recall my dad ever saying he fought in the war or got his foot shot off!"

"But it's all true," said Emma. "And more. There are special clubs for people who keep pigeons. And there's even a Pigeon Hall of Fame for the bravest and most famous of us."

"Now I *know* you're kidding!" Clarence scoffed.

"You don't know *anything!*" Emma shouted. "This is our *heritage!* Just because you spend all your time on this ledge, or scrounging in the streets for castoffs, you assume *all* pigeons do the same. But there's a greater world out there, Clarence. And we pigeons are part of it!"

Clarence was surprised by his wife's sudden intensity. He'd never heard her speak that way, or refer to him in such insulting terms, and he didn't care for her new haughty attitude. He began to wonder if sending Emma to the library had been such a great idea after all!

But it was too late to do anything about it. With the

exception of Sundays, Emma continued to fly there every morning, and not return till almost four-thirty. She ignored all chores and wifely duties, explaining her "research" was far more important, and leaving Clarence alone to forage and care for the children.

The woman returned to the table by the window every day for more than a week. At the end of that time, Emma had gained a complete knowledge of pigeons from the beginning of recorded history to the present.

With mixed emotions, Emma watched the woman finally close the cover on the 900-page volume on pigeons. Their mutual education complete, Emma knew her companion would no longer return to the table by the window. How she longed to call out and ask her to reopen the book and read it once more, starting from page one. Sadly, she watched the woman gather up her notes, turn in the book, and leave the library.

Emma decided there was no point in returning to the library the next day, for no other topic could possibly be of equal interest to her. She didn't discuss her new-found knowledge with her husband any more, sensing his disapproval. But she'd come to a startling realization regarding what she'd learned.

Apart from pigeons having a noble history, they were quite different from most other birds. That's why they weren't found in the jungles or uninhabited deserts, but in the big cities of the world. The pigeon is one of the few animals to inhabit man's immediate human community. The relationship between man and pigeon started at the end of the Ice Age and has continued to the present. The pigeon is the constant companion of man. Man's buildings, highways, bridges, and sculptures afford it ideal housing. Whatever man's future may be, it is certain the pigeon will accompany him into it.

At long last, Emma knew what that strange stirring inside her truly meant. She'd been living her life all wrong! She and her friends thought of people merely as food suppliers, forgetting their great common heritage. *That's* why she'd been shunned and looked down upon.

Well, it was time to change all that!

Armed with this new knowledge, her duty seemed quite clear!

CHAPTER THIRTEEN

*H*ey, Em," said Clarence, kicking away
the debris from the previous night's dinner. "I thought
you said you'd finished your 'research' a few days ago."

"Oh, I did," she said.

"Then how about a good clean-up job today? This
roost's a regular wreck."

"Oh, I'll be much too busy for that," she said, combing out her feathers with the end of her beak. "Perhaps
Roscoe could come by and help you straighten things
up."

"Roscoe hasn't been coming by lately," he said accusingly. "Not since you made that nasty crack about him plucking out pigeon feathers. You really hurt his feelings, Em."

Emma finished combing and fluffed herself out. "I only spoke the truth, dear. Besides, sparrows are a noisy bunch at best. And Roscoe's the worst of the lot. I don't see why you bother with him. We pigeons have a reputation to live up to, you know."

Clarence glared at his wife as she continued her grooming. "If you ask me, it's the other way around."

"Whatever do you mean, dear?"

"Ever since you got so high-and-mighty, I've been trying to *live down* your reputation. You've offended just about everyone we know. Like yesterday, when my pal Harry the Starling dropped by for dinner. Boy, did you let him have it!"

"I merely told him what I'd learned about his species," said Emma. "Starlings build slovenly nests, they're dirty and noisy, and they've driven thousands of woodpeckers, flycatchers, and flickers from gardens and nest holes. It was right there in the book."

"Maybe so," said Clarence, "but poor old Harry's never *seen* a garden or nest hole. And he doesn't even know what a flicker or flycatcher is! Besides, he's no noisier than most of your girl friends."

"On that you may be right," said Emma, glancing at her reflection in the Dixie Cup of water. "I've already planned to gather some of the girls together one evening and teach them proper pigeon etiquette. They really shouldn't spend so much time by the garbage cans. It doesn't seem proper. But right now, I have more important things to do."

"But I thought you, me, and the kids could take a dip in the sprinklers this morning," sulked Clarence. "Summer's almost over, and they'll be turning them off soon. Besides, you haven't played with the kids in ages."

"Oh, they're quite happy playing all day with little Priscilla and Nan," said Emma. "I'm sure Monica wouldn't mind keeping an eye on them again. You know how she enjoys those homey little chores."

Clarence was silent a moment, fondly remembering the time when Emma had enjoyed those "homey little chores." "Could we at least have lunch together, like in the old days?" he asked.

"Afraid not dear. Perhaps you could pick up some dinner for me, though. Some rice or oats maybe."

"Oats?" shouted Clarence. "Where the heck am I supposed to find oats?"

"Well, pigeon breeders feed it to their stock all the time," she said matter-of-factly. "It's very good for our flight feathers I think. Carrier pigeons must be kept in tip-top shape, you know."

"Yeah, well if I fly past a mounted policeman in the park, maybe I can steal his horse's feedbag!" he said sarcastically.

"That would be just fine, dear," said Emma, flicking some dust from her claws.

"For crying out loud, Em! You're no carrier pigeon!" Clarence fumed. "When are you gonna stop living in that daydream? You've already got the kids acting like nuts—limping around, pretending they're shot in the legs. Filling their heads with all those fairy tales. When are you going to wake up?"

"You couldn't be more wrong," Emma argued, posturing dramatically. "I *used* to be in a dull daydream. But now, my eyes are wide open to reality."

"Well, if they're so wide open," said Clarence, fluttering off the ledge, "go find your own oats!"

Then he flew in the direction of the playground.

Emma shook her head in disgust. He'd change his mind soon enough, she thought, when she'd proven she was right. But there was no time to lose. Once she'd found a mission important enough to show herself worthy of the carrier pigeon's heritage, Clarence would be convinced she wasn't daydreaming.

She'd be working at a disadvantage, though, since carrier pigeons had prescribed assignments and instructions, and she'd have to find her own. But that made it more challenging. With the millions of people in New York City, there must be lots of them requiring her services. She'd fly out and find some right away!

Emma quickly flew off toward Broadway, in search of a person in distress. She didn't have to look far. At

89th Street, she saw a man running from the entrance of a card shop, waving a small brown bag.

"Madam!" he shouted up the street. "You forgot your package!"

What a perfect opportunity to begin training, thought Emma. It wasn't an important mission, but at least it was a start. She swooped down and snatched the bag from the startled man's hand. Now which "Madam" was she to give it to? There were several women hurrying down the block so she fluttered by each one, the small package stuck in her beak.

One woman screamed when she saw Emma flapping in front of her face; another swatted her away with the back of her hand and quickly walked on. But the third woman stopped a moment.

"My goodness," she said, noticing what Emma had clutched in her beak. "That's my package. That bird stole my package. It took it right out of my purse. Give it back."

The woman snatched the bag from Emma's beak without even a "thank you," then stamped off down the street. But Emma was undaunted. One thoughtless woman couldn't dampen her enthusiasm. Flying further downtown, she noticed some young people seated in the center of the sidewalk on 79th Street. They had a small table stacked with leaflets in front of them.

"Please read what our candidate thinks on important world issues!" a girl shouted.

"There's only one person who can stop pollution, crime in the streets, overcrowding," a young man cried, as he waved a stack of leaflets above his head. "Find out who this one man is!"

Most of the pedestrians passed right by, giving no notice to the young people.

"How can we save our city?" shouted another girl. "All those interested in civic problems, read this and vote YES on Election Day!"

Now here was a truly important cause, thought Emma. A perfect opportunity for her to help. Everyone should be taking those leaflets and reading them, instead of passing those young people by.

So Emma swooped down, grabbed a stack of leaflets in her beak and began flying around the street, dropping them onto people's heads. She even tried stuffing a few down inside men's shirts, but that proved too difficult.

"What the heck's going on?" one man yelled, picking a leaflet from his hat.

"Probably some crazy campaign publicity," said another. "Some guys'll do anything to get elected!"

"That's right," agreed a fat woman, picking a leaflet from her shopping bag. "And these young radical kids'll do anything for attention!"

As they threw the papers to the sidewalk, Emma picked them up again and dropped them on someone else. Why didn't they understand? she thought.

She'd created quite a crowd in the center of the sidewalk by the time the policeman wandered by. Emma was sure he'd come to help her distribute the leaflets, so she grabbed another pile and dropped them on the officer's cap.

"What's the matter here?" he asked, sizing up the situation.

"It's that bird, officer," one of the girls shouted. "It's taken all our campaign literature."

"It's some crazy Communist plot!" shouted the fat woman. "These kids want to force us to read their lies!"

"Ought to be a law against birds in the city!" grumbled an old man, trying to swat Emma with his cane.

Emma flew off just in time, leaving the policeman, the young campaigners, and the passersby in the center of a heated, noisy, mixed-up argument.

Being a carrier pigeon in Manhattan was going to be more difficult than she'd expected!

CHAPTER FOURTEEN

*E*mma's two failures only served to strengthen her determination. The fact that a small group of stupid people misunderstood her noble motives was no reason for giving up!

So the next day, she ventured out again, this time heading further downtown. She flew down along the West Side Highway. When she reached 59th Street, she saw the large ocean liners docked at the West Side piers, but no longer yearned to set sail to those far away places. Her "work" was more important.

There was a large liner, *The Franconia*, about to lift

anchor, and dozens of people were on hand to see her off. The last person had just boarded the gangplank, and crowds were waving goodbye, laughing and smiling, some crying. But one little woman in the crowd was shouting and waving a slip of paper.

"Beatrice!" she shouted. "You've forgotten to take down Uncle Arthur's address in Kensington."

Naturally, Emma quickly dove to the rescue, snatching the note from the little woman. With paper in beak, she began searching the deck for Beatrice. But just as before, confusion followed when the passengers saw a pigeon flapping around in front of their faces.

"Aren't pigeons bad luck on ships?" one lady asked, swatting Emma with her purse.

"Oh no," said another. "You're thinking of the albatross. You know. That story about the sailor with the dead bird hung around his neck?"

Emma didn't stop to hear the rest of the story. She dropped Beatrice's note on the deck and quickly flew away, leaving a crowd of angry, fist-shaking passengers behind.

She flew toward Central Park, and there she saw a young man seated on the grass by Belvedere Lake, busily writing. A gust of wind swept by and sent his papers fluttering in all directions. Of course, Emma helped him retrieve them. Unfortunately, she snatched up too many pages in her beak and as she flew over the lake, most of them dropped into the water.

"Hey, you crazy bird," the young man yelled. "You just drowned my manuscript."

Emma sighed and decided to call it a day.

By the end of the week, Emma had "helped" over a dozen people, but as yet not one had appreciated it. She consoled herself with the thought that she was at least gaining knowledge about Manhattan. She already knew almost every building, statue, and park around town. She knew the warehouse and factory district of the Lower West Side, mid-Manhattan with its busy intersections and steel and glass office buildings, the quiet East Side streets with their charming brownstones. And everywhere she went, she surveyed the landmarks closely, taking in every detail, as she looked for her big "mission."

Then one clear, fateful day at the end of August, Destiny finally smiled on her. While flying by Park Avenue and 68th Street, she found what she'd been searching for.

From inside an opened window of an old ornate building, there came the sound of a woman crying. The woman was seated at an antique oak desk, her head buried in her hands. There was a man standing over her, looking angry and upset.

"How could you *do* such a thing!!" he shouted. "You know how important those papers are! They're vital to our diplomatic mission. And you let Mrs. Paul go off without them!"

The woman's sobs grew louder. "I'm so sorry, Mr. Romanelli," she whimpered. "I meant to give Mrs. Paul the papers. See, they're right here on my desk. I just forgot. I realize it's urgent, but what can I do now?"

The man snatched the papers up from the desk and started pacing about the room.

"There's nothing anyone can do now," he growled. "Mrs. Paul has gone, and I don't know where to contact her!"

Emma sat on the window ledge, listening to every word. Yes, Fate had finally guided her to a true "mission"!

But who were these people and why were those papers so important? Glancing over at the plaque on the front of the building, her questions were answered. THE ITALIAN CONSULATE.

So that was it! Emma had read all about consulates and Consul Generals at the library. A Consul General was a very important foreign diplomat, and the building he lived in was called the Consulate. All major countries had consulates in the United States and technically they were considered foreign soil.

So the people in this building were from Italy . . . home of Leonardo . . . the country in which the carrier pigeon G.I. Joe had fought so bravely. And those vital papers were probably some international treaty. If Mrs. Paul didn't get them in time, maybe there'd be another war! This could be Emma's big opportunity to do what G.I. Joe had done years before. Only this time, she wouldn't just be saving a battalion. She'd be saving a whole country!

The man was still pacing the floor, the papers in his hand.

"If only we knew where to find Mrs. Paul," he said again.

Emma's heart beat faster, as she suddenly remembered a downtown building she'd passed that morning. It stood out in her mind like a beacon. She and she alone knew where to find Mrs. Paul! She would carry the vital papers to her and save the entire Italian Government from ruin!

Quickly, she flew through the window and fluttered about the room. Startled, the woman jumped up from her desk, and the man began wacking her with the handful of papers. But Emma hovered over his head, trying to grab the papers with her beak. He swatted her again, and she felt a dull pain across her chest.

"What's this insane pigeon doing?" the man shouted, wacking her again.

The woman started running about the office, looking for something to hit Emma with while the man flailed his arms in the air. Emma swooped down, grabbed the papers up, and flew out the window.

"Come back here, you filthy bird!" the man shouted after her. "Those papers are important!"

But Emma flew higher and higher, until soon she was

out of sight. The papers hung heavy in her beak and her chest stung a bit, but still she flew, high up over the buildings and rooftops and park, until she was on the West Side. She headed downtown toward the warehouse district, searching for the building she'd spotted earlier. Yes, there it was, coming into view—a dingy, brown warehouse with big letters painted across one side: MRS. PAUL'S.

She peeked in all the windows on all the floors. Seeing no one inside any of the rooms, she came to rest on the roof. There she carefully slipped the papers from her beak, rested them by her feet, and waited. When would Mrs. Paul come? What did the papers say? Should she read them?

She glanced at them, but they were in a foreign language. Italian, no doubt. She waited some more. Mrs. Paul was sure to arrive shortly. And when she did, wouldn't she be thrilled? Wouldn't she think Emma brave? Wouldn't she want to give her a medal?

But Mrs. Paul didn't come. Emma sat on the roof for what seemed like hours, but no one came. Once a delivery truck stopped in front of the building. Would Mrs. Paul get out? The driver opened the gate, dropped a large carton at the rear entrance, closed the gate again, then drove away. Still Emma waited.

Before long, dusk started to settle on the city. Emma knew it was too late for her to return home that evening. She would have to sit on the roof all night. So she sat on the pile of papers as lovingly as if they were one of her own eggs. Mrs. Paul would come soon, she told herself, shivering slightly. Mrs. Paul *would* come! She just knew it!

What poor Emma didn't know was that the sign plastered against the side of the building was part of a very old advertisement, almost worn away by time and weather.

It used to say: MRS. PAUL'S FROZEN FISH STICKS. TRY THEM TONIGHT.

CHAPTER FIFTEEN

*I*t had been the darkest, loneliest night of Emma's life, filled with strange city sounds she'd never been aware of before. No food. No water. No sleep. No Mrs. Paul!

When morning finally dawned, Emma had given up all hope of ever seeing the mysterious woman. With heavy wings and a heavier heart, she fluttered down to the back entrance of the warehouse and slipped the vital papers under the rope of a carton lying there. Perhaps Mrs. Paul would come by some other day. At any rate, she, Emma, had completed *her* part of the mission. No

to the small shape of her son. He was lying on his side on a bed of twigs and branches, his head resting on a rolled-up paper napkin. One battered wing rested against his chest and two of the claws on his right leg were bruised and bloodied. Emma felt a sudden dizziness when she saw the flaming red splotch of broken tendons and the soft gray baby feathers matted down with dried blood.

Monica Pigeon was seated beside him, cooing softly and applying wet tissue paper to his wounds.

"My poor baby boy," sobbed Emma. "My poor, sweet baby boy!"

Willie turned his head and moaned softly. "It's not so bad, Ma. Don't worry."

"He's coming along just fine," said Monica reassuringly. "He had us worried for a while last night, but. . . ."

"I kept callin' for ya, Ma," said Willie. "All night long, I kept callin' for ya. But ya never came. Why didn't ya come, Ma?"

"If only I'd *known!*" sobbed Emma. "How could such a dreadful thing *happen?*"

"He was playing with Priscilla and Nan in the park," Monica explained, "when all of a sudden, he got this crazy notion to . . ."

"It wasn't a notion," said Willie, trying to sit up. But the sudden flash of pain in his wing made his head fall back onto the paper pillow. "I was playing carrier pi-

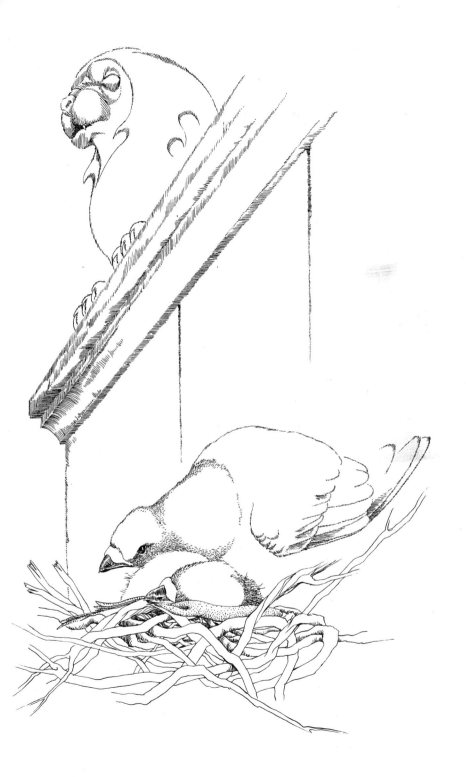

geon, Ma. This big boy in the playground dropped some papers on the grass. So I flew down to pick them up. I tried to help him, Ma. Like those birds in the stories you've been telling us. But he was a bad boy. He took out his slingshot and started hitting me with stones."

"Now, now," soothed Monica, dropping another cold tissue on his wounds. "Try to forget it. You're a very brave pigeon, and I'm sure your mother's proud of you."

"Are you, Ma?" asked Willie, a pleading look in his eyes. "That carrier pigeon stuff is so important to you. I wanted to make you proud of me. Did I do it good, like Cher Ami?"

"Of course, my darling," whispered Emma, her eyes welling up with tears. "You're my brave little boy. After all, this was just your first mission. You'll do much better the next time. When you're all better, I'll teach you how. But now, I'm going to take you home and. . . ."

"I'm afraid he can't be moved for several days," said Monica. "He's quite comfortable here. And I don't mind taking care of him. He's become like one of the family lately."

"Yeah, Aunt Monica's been swell," said Willie. "She stayed up with me all night and cooed in my ear. She told me lots of stories about the big building she was born on near Columbus Avenue. And she put wet tissues

on my wing to make the hurt go away. She likes doin'
stuff like that. Wasn't I lucky she was around?"

"Where were you last night, Emma?" asked Monica,
trying not to sound accusing.

"I was downtown," she said somberly. "On a vital
government mission. You see, no sacrifice is too great
for those who follow the call of duty. But if I'd
known. . . ."

Clarence flew by just then, landing next to his son's
sickbed.

"How's my little fella today?" he asked softly.

"Much better, Dad," said Willie. "Monica says her
baby brother got hurt once, even worse than me. And
she took care of him, too. For *three weeks*. Do ya think
I'll be sick that long? Well, I don't really mind. Monica
says when I'm all better, she's gonna give me a surprise
present. She found it in the sandbox and she's saving it
for me. Monica says. . . ."

Emma turned away from her son, momentarily struck
by an emptiness far greater than any she'd ever known
before.

CHAPTER SIXTEEN

*E*mma decided to postpone all further flights until her son had completely recovered. She visited him every afternoon, reading him the last three pages of *The Little Engine That Could*, over and over again, constantly reassuring him his first flight had been commendable and that he'd do much better on future missions.

"Just keep saying those words over to yourself, Willie," she instructed. "I think I can. I think I can. And you'll do just fine. Perhaps we'll even start flying out together. We could be a mother-and-son team!"

"Do I have to fly out again?" asked Willie.

"Well, not for a while, of course," said Emma. "We'll wait till you're all better."

True, Emma was envious of the affection that Willie lavished on Monica, and the attention Monica gave him in return. And she was aware of Clarence's constant stony silences. But that would change the moment Willie was well again. In the meantime, Emma returned to homelier chores, but found the dusting and cleaning and foraging thankless tasks, lacking the excitement of her challenging new career. But until her son was able to join her in future flights, she was determined to place motherhood above all else.

On the fourth day after Willie's accident, Freddie the Cat returned from Martha's Vineyard. He wasn't back more than a few hours before he was out on the fire escape *psssstting* as usual. With a backlog of two months' mail and magazines, naturally Emma was the first person he wanted to see.

"Hey, Em," he called. "Come down and tell me all about your summer in Soot City."

"It's had its ups and downs, Freddie," said Emma, fluttering to the seventh floor.

"Yeah," he said. "Roscoe peeped in my window this morning and told me about your kid's accident. That's real rough, Em. Hope he's feelin' better."

"We're a brave breed, Willie," said Emma philosophically. "We come from noble and hearty stock."

"Yeah, well that don't help much when someone shoots a rock past your rear end! I've had my share of close calls from slingshots myself. There's some kid across the court who's got a drawer full of 'em. The mayor oughta outlaw 'em."

"How was *your* summer, Freddie?" asked Emma.

"Not bad. Not bad at all," he said, in between paw licks. "I was all wrong about that Vineyard place. I had a real neat setup there—miles of beach, cool salt water, fresh clams and crabs for dinner every night. It's gonna take a few days for me ta get all the sand out of my paddy-paws, though. And I better hurry it up, cause the folks are talkin' about given' me a bath. Can ya believe it? Didya ever hear of anyone givin' a cat a bath? With *bubbles*, no less! I swear the old lady is getting nuts! She spent the whole summer sittin' under a beach umbrella on the patio. Never even put her big feet in the water! She might as well have stayed at home and sat in the closet!"

"Well, we all have our preferences," said Emma. "What you consider strange, may be ideal for another type of individual."

Freddie paused from his paw-washing and looked at her. "You seem kinda different, Em," he said.

Emma smiled. "I was hoping you'd notice," she said. "I've had much heartache and sorrow these past few months, but I think I can safely say I'm quite a different bird from the one you previously knew."

"Yeah," said Freddie. "I noticed you talkin' kinda *weird*. Ya still *read* though, don't ya?"

"Why, of course. In fact, I'm now considered quite an intellectual pigeon."

"Great!" he said, jumping up. He crawled inside his window, returning with a pile of papers and letters in his mouth, and plunked them on the fire escape.

"This is just a drop in the bucket," he said, grinning. "The place was flooded with mail when we got back. Look through it for me will ya? But skip the bills and junk. I don't bother with the old folks' financial problems."

Emma sorted through the collection with her beak. She read an invitation to a baby shower, a thank you note, a letter from someone named Herbert Woodstock, telling all about his gallbladder operation, and two scenic postcards.

"Hey, glance through that paper called *The Manhattanite*," said Freddie, pointing with his paw. "It's one of those neighborhood freebie jobs. Tells all about what's goin' on on the West Side. The old folks read an article in there once about someone wanting ta tear down this building. It had them pretty scared for a while."

Emma turned the pages with her beak. On page three of the newspaper, she saw a photograph of pigeons that caught her eye.

"I wonder what this is about," she said, reading the opening sentence:

. . . Residents of the West Side have been suddenly plagued by the curious antics of a group of our fellow New Yorkers, the pigeons. . . .

"Sounds interesting," said Freddie. "Read it to me."

. . . Several people have complained of being harassed by a curiously vicious band of birds. There's no way of knowing how large a number of pigeons are involved in these persecutions, as the incidents happen sporadically and the witnesses are always emotional. But many residents of the area have been molested by the pesky creatures. One woman was assaulted at midday on 79th Street. Another young man had a valuable manuscript ripped from his hands in Central Park. Nor has this bird mania been restricted to the West Side. Employees of the Italian Consulate on Park Avenue claimed marauding pigeons ransacked their private files. Luckily, duplicate documents of the stolen papers exist.

City residents are at a loss to explain the sudden, vicious attacks, but all insist they stop as soon as possible. It's common knowledge that the pigeon population of Manhattan is upsettlingly large. People have long been accus-

tomed to the creatures fouling our buildings and infesting our streets, but have taken their existence in stride with the usual tough-hearted acceptance of New Yorkers.

The sudden onslaught of these attacks, however, has resuscitated some strong feelings regarding the health hazards these birds create. It brings to mind the many newspaper articles that periodically emanate from large cities. First, there was the Salmonella exposé in the 1930s. Then equine encephalitis, psittacosic-ornithosis, Newcastle disease, toxoplasmosis, and finally cryptococcosis.

City health departments continually try to do something about the overabundant park pigeons, but to no avail. Now, it seems private citizens are determined to take the matter into their own hands. Several people have suggested dropping poison pellets on top of buildings and on sidewalks, to eliminate large numbers of pigeons. But potential danger to children and pets would seem to dissuade citizens from such tactics.

Personally, this reporter has always felt a certain fondness for pigeons, having worked with racing homers during World War II, at which time they were referred to as "winged telegraphs." However, electronic devices have all but taken the place of pigeons in modern warfare. In any event, these noble fighting birds bear no resemblance to the common street scavengers of Manhattan. . . .

Emma didn't finish the rest of the article. She dropped the newspaper and began stamping on it with her claws.

"Lies! Lies! All lies!" she shouted.

"Hey, cut that out," Freddie shouted. "The old folks ain't finished readin' that yet!"

"I don't care," she said, stamping on the paper again, until it slipped through the fire escape grating and floated to the sidewalk.

"You sure are actin' wacky today," said Freddie. "Just 'cause some guy wrote about a bunch of cuckoo birds, you act like he was talkin' about *you*."

"Well, he was," she said. "Yes, it's true. *I'm* the filthy, vicious band of birds! No, I mean it's not true! I'm *not* a street scavenger. I'm not, do you hear? Everybody wants me to believe it, but I won't. *I won't!*"

Emma darted off the ledge and swiftly flew up to the roof, leaving Freddie with his mouth wide open, his brows knit together, scratching the top of his head with his paw.

CHAPTER SEVENTEEN

*N*ow calm down, Em," said Clarence. "You're talking so fast, I can hardly understand a word. You're getting your feathers ruffled over nothing. Just because some fellow wrote those silly things in the paper, doesn't mean. . . ."

"But they're *lies*," she insisted. "I don't carry diseases. There isn't a day goes by I don't take my morning bath in the Dixie Cup. And I've taught the children to do the same. You *know* that, Clarence. Oh, you should have heard the horrible names of those diseases. How could I have such things? I've never even heard of them! And now, they may drop poison in the streets, endangering all our lives. Do you think we should keep the children at home? It's not safe for any of us to fly around any more. Perhaps we should *hide* the children!"

"I love hide-and-seek," chirped Maude, coming around the corner of the ledge, "only Willie's not well enough to play yet. But maybe he could watch us. Why don't I go hide by the Fireman's Monument, and you and Daddy can. . . ."

"Don't you dare leave this roost again," Emma shouted.

"It's not as bad as all that," said Clarence. "Why frighten the kids? New Yorkers are always running off at the mouth about cleaning up the streets. But they never do. They enjoy living in a mess. It's part of their culture."

"Don't talk to me about their *culture*," fumed Emma. "After all I've tried to do for them."

"Well, maybe you should have been doing more for *us*, and not been worrying so much about *them*," said Clarence. "Why don't you be a *real* homing pigeon for a change. *Stay home!* From all you've told me, nobody would be dropping poison anythings, if you hadn't started flying around the city on your lame-brain missions."

"You've never understood my motives," said Emma, turning her face away to fight back tears. "I only wanted to better myself. So we wouldn't all be called street scavengers for the rest of our lives. I wanted people to *respect* me."

"So you figured you'd spend your time stealing people's stuff and maybe getting your legs shot off? Look what that crazy thinking's done to poor Willie over there."

"Lower your voice," said Emma, going over to where her son was napping in the alcove. "This is his first day back in his own roost, and I won't have him upset. I did what I had to do. How else could I get humans to respect me?"

"For crying out loud, Em," said Clarence, walking a safe distance from his son's sick bed. "It seems to me you have to respect *yourself* first. I may be a foolish kind of guy at times, but even I could have told you that. Oh, I know you get fed up with all my talk about food and restaurants, and you don't approve of all my friends. But that's me. And I'm not ashamed of it. So what if Monica's a stay-at-home and Roscoe's sort of loud and Sanford's kind of grumpy. That's their nature, and they're happy that way. And you're my wife—Willie and Maude's mother. That should be enough to satisfy you. Quit trying to be somebody else."

"But I'm *more* than that," Emma insisted. "Much more. After all I've seen and experienced, how could I possibly go back to being that dull drab pigeon I used to be? I refuse to do it!"

"But we loved you that way, Mom," said Maude.

"We like you dull and ordinary. That's what moms are supposed to be. Us kids don't like moms with surprises."

"But I want more of life," said Emma. "I haven't suffered all summer just to go back to being the same old Emma. That point you made about self-respect may be true, Clarence. But there's more to it than that. *You* have to respect me, too. And you don't. You've been against me from the moment I started getting culture. And I don't understand it. After all, you were the one who first encouraged me to read and discover new things. If it hadn't been for you, I never would have learned about our pigeon heritage."

"But don't you see?" said Clarence. "People don't *care* about our heritage. What if we are part of some noble family of war heroes? So what? If people are nuts about carrier pigeons, it's because they can *use* them. No self-respecting pigeon would get himself shot to pieces unless he was *made* to do it. Personally, I'm proud to be a city bird. Maybe I eat in the streets and sleep in the soot, but I *chose* it. And I wouldn't change it for a chest full of medals."

Emma sighed wistfully. She had to admit Clarence made a good deal of sense. She'd never gotten any real pleasure out of being a carrier pigeon, and certainly no honor.

"I guess you're right," she said. "But that doesn't change the way I feel. If I can't be respected for my heritage, I have to be respected for myself. I'm not just your wife and Willie and Maude's mother. I'm *me*."

Clarence was silent a moment, considering what Emma had said.

"That kind of deal has to work *both* ways, Em," he said finally. "After all, you've got to learn to respect me, too. I love the city streets, filth and all. And I don't intend to change."

"And I love my books," said Emma haughtily. "And if you had an open mind, you might learn to love them, too. Perhaps I could give up my carrier pigeon dreams if I felt you and the children at least shared some of my other interests."

Clarence walked toward his wife and stared at her with a thoughtful expression. "Do you really mean that?" he asked.

"Of course I do," said Emma.

"Well then, honey, I think we've just made ourselves a deal. This family is about to become a regular Mutual Admiration Society!"

CHAPTER EIGHTEEN

Cool autumn breezes swept through the city, blowing away the stale hazy air and cooling the cement sidewalks. Crab apples and burrs began to fall from the trees along the Drive, and leaves turned from faded greens to golds and russets. Gone were the long lazy days for picnics on the grass, and ice cream wagons were replaced by hot pretzel and chestnut vendors.

Gone, too, were the threats of poison pellets in the streets. Once the mysterious "pigeon attacks" ceased, city dwellers again simply ignored their feathered neighbors.

Willie had quite recovered, nursed back to health by his loving, watchful mother. Emma had sat by his side day and night, feeding him, changing his bandages, and assuring him he'd never ever have to fly another mission—unless he truly wanted to. Willie felt quite relieved when he learned he could abandon the weighty burdens of the carrier pigeon, and happily returned to racing with his friends and playing with his piece of rubber ball.

As the season slowly changed, so did the quality of Emma's life on the ledge. She and Clarence kept their promise to one another and began a true campaign of mutual understanding.

Emma lost no time in asking for and getting several delicious new recipes from Monica Pigeon. Every Saturday, Emma foraged for Clarence's favorite dishes, and that night they'd have a quiet dinner, just the two of them, on their private terrace, with candlelight provided by the passing highway headlights.

Each Sunday, Emma cared for the children, while Clarence spent the entire day "hanging around the old haunts" with his buddies. He usually returned home, waddling a bit, having gorged himself on too much pizza and too many hamburger buns. But Emma never scolded.

Once a week, the family flew down to the service entrance of their 99th Street building to browse through the pile of newspapers and magazines stacked for pick-up by the Sanitation Department. They'd all sit in the alleyway, while Emma gave rudimentary reading lessons. Willie was quick to pick up the knack and got quite involved in leafing through sports magazines; while Maude spent most of her time with her beak buried in the fashion ads. Clarence had a bit more difficulty and usually settled for the Sunday comic section of *The Daily News*. On occasion, though, he'd struggle through the gourmet column of *The New York Times*—but only if Emma promised to try to approximate the dishes. And Emma, of course, spent her time reading the book reviews.

Every Tuesday, Clarence took full charge of the children and housekeeping, while Emma spent the day at the 42nd Street Library. Thanks to the undying curiosity of scholarly New Yorkers, she learned much about a variety of topics, including flora and fauna. Before long, she was able to identify every tree and bush on Riverside Drive. She also memorized the batting averages of every baseball player in the Major Leagues, which was a constant source of delight to Willie.

As for other subjects, Emma's knowledge of electrical contracting, torpedo boats and the natural resources of Albania were of little use to her. But she found her education in Egyptology, the English Reformation, and Oriental cultures quite fascinating. In addition, she discovered the location of every historical site and museum in Manhattan, whereupon Clarence promised faithfully to take her to see them all—sooner or later.

On Wednesdays and Fridays during October and November, the family flew to Central Park to chat with the fall migratory birds visiting there. They built up some lively friendships with a magpie, a mockingbird, and a Swainson's thrush. The "out-of-towners" told all about their homes in Alaska, Wyoming, and Quebec, and were always most impressed to learn Emma knew even more about their habitats than they did. Thanks to Freddie the Cat, Emma was kept constantly supplied with back issues of *National Geographic*, and knew much about the various areas in the world, from frozen tundra to desert salt flats.

Clarence was finally forced to admit that the colorful migrants were for the most part polite and friendly and their stories interesting, but to properly balance his children's education, he felt it his duty to extoll the beauties and excitement of the big city as well. He took the family on tours of Chinatown, Greenwich Village, the New Fulton Fish Market, and Inwood Hill Park; and had already planned winter trips to Rockefeller Center Skating Rink and the ski slope in Van Cortlandt Park.

Roscoe the Sparrow was puzzled at his best friend's sudden interest in sightseeing, but after Clarence told him of the tantalizing scraps of fried noodles and dumplings he'd sampled in Chinatown, and the great quantities of hot chestnuts ice skaters were likely to drop on the ice in winter, Roscoe grew interested himself.

Old Sanford Pigeon often criticized his neighbors for "flittering around town, wasting good time with your beaks stuffed in books." Emma tried to explain how informative a good book could be—how she'd learned that Oriental societies revere and venerate their eldest members, realizing the old can impart valuable knowledge and wisdom to the young. Sanford only grumbled, "You don't have to snoop in books to find that out. *I've* known that for years!" But for the most part, Emma's friends had to admit her family's new life style lent a measure of color and excitement to the neighborhood.

And each night before her children nodded off to sleep, Emma would tell them a story. Sometimes, it would be from the beat-up little paperback book of fairy tales she'd found stuffed in the sandbox one day. But usually, Willie and Maude preferred to hear the story of Leonardo da Vinci and how he had attempted to master the art of flying.

"Not *that* again?" Emma would ask, secretly delighted.

"Oh yes, Ma," Willie would plead, "tell us that one."

And so, after the proper dramatic pause, she would:

"Long ago, in a place called Italy," she began, "there lived a very wise and talented man named Leonardo da Vinci. He was the wisest and most brilliant man in all the ancient world. He painted great pictures on the walls of famous buildings, made beautiful statues, and filled many books with ideas for inventions and theories of city planning and anatomy. But Leonardo was never completely satisfied. He wanted to do one thing more. He longed to fly. So he designed a giant pair of wings— a pair of wings bigger and more magnificent than any bird could ever hope to have. He built these wings from a network of wooden pieces, coated it with cloth, then glued on a layer of feathers, planning to attach it to the shoulders of a man. When this was finished, he wrote in his notebook, 'From Mount Cecere the famous bird will take flight, which will fill the world with its great renown.' "

Though Willie and Maude remembered quite well how the story ended, they would always ask the same question. "Did it work, Ma? Did Leonardo figure out how to fly?"

"No, children," Emma would continue, "as legend has it, a servant of Leonardo's took those wings and ran to the top of the highest hill. When a breeze came up, he began flapping those wings harder and harder, then hurled himself out into space. But the man fell to the bottom of the hill, his leg broken. The wings were smashed to pieces, and Leonardo never made another pair. So you see, children, even Leonardo—painter, sculptor, musician, architect, scientist, one of the greatest geniuses of all time—could not learn the secret of flying. He never managed to do what the commonest of pigeons can do whenever it wishes. He never mastered the great gift of flight!"

Then the children would smile and sigh, and after a while, drift off to a pleasureful sleep.

In addition to all these activities, Emma initiated a weekly "scavenger hunt" for her family. She took the children up and down the side streets to forage for treasure. They had already found a shiny black marble, a postcard with a picture of Nefertiti, a plaster cherry from a ladies' straw hat, a smiley-face button with the pin missing but the front intact, and two wooden pencils with the points still on. A special corner of the ledge was set aside for the children's discoveries. There they spent many happy hours chattering and making up stories about where the items had come from and about the people who'd dropped them.

One afternoon, while Willie was rolling his pencil over a scrap of construction paper he'd found in the park, Emma noticed something quite extraordinary.

"CLARENCE!" she shouted, "Come over here and see what little Willie's done!"

Clarence ambled over to look at his son's project.

"I don't see anything," he said, nodding his head from side to side.

"But look," said Emma excitedly. "Willie's made the letter *W* with his pencil!"

"So?"

"Well, he's *reading* so well. Now it looks as if he's learning to *write*, too. No one in our family has ever

learned how to write before. That's quite a unique talent. At this rate, if he really has the gift and works at it, he could become a member of the Pigeon Hall of Fame!"

Clarence gave his wife a long, questioning look. He sincerely hoped she was only joking!

Mary Anderson is a native New Yorker, born in Manhattan, and has lived there all her life. She and her husband, illustrator Carl Anderson, and their three daughters live in a large old building on Riverside Drive, not unlike the one she writes about in this book. As a matter of fact, the building across the street from theirs has a cornice with twelve fierce lions decorating its facade and is the actual home of Emma and her family. Mrs. Anderson and her children are frequent, longtime visitors to the 97th Street Playground, where Clarence is so fond of "scrounging." One day, as her daughter fed the pigeons, she noticed one bird, a bit aloof and different from the rest. She decided to use her as the main character in this book. Of course, the author can't be positive, but perhaps this pigeon, too, knew how to read.

Mrs. Anderson is the author of one other published book: Matilda Investigates.